"How did I do?
inspection?"

Still meeting his gaze .... You
did fine, obviously."

The gaze he slid her made bells and whistles go
off in her body. Her body buzzed, and her legs
tightened in response to the hint of a smile on his
lips. Smiling, she'd decided, was overrated. Better
than a smile was the start of one. The way it began
in the eyes, moving slowly.

It felt like a teaser of "coming attractions."

Damn it!

She looked away first, too unnerved by the blatant
invitation in his eyes.

"Okay! I see everything is good in here. I'll make
her a bottle for when she wakes up and I can take
her next door."

She thought she heard him mutter "chicken" as she
quietly walked away.

Dear Reader,

Welcome home to Charming, Texas. I hope you stay awhile. I've always wanted to write about a baby left on a doorstep and it's finally time. Who would do such a thing? Why? And more importantly, perhaps, who would not immediately call the authorities? They better have a good reason! Don't worry—he does.

Maribel Del Toro is back in Charming for a vacation after falling in love with the area while attending her brother's wedding. She rents a cottage by the beach and prepares to practice mindfulness. Among the peace and quiet of the Gulf Coast, she will teach herself to cook and enjoy reading books. She doesn't think the surly neighbor to her side will be much interference as he's mostly ignoring her. The cowboy surfer is good-looking but definitely not her type. Especially not when he accuses her of leaving her baby on the doorstep!

It isn't long before these two grumps agree to watch the baby for two weeks and get to know they have more in common than they ever would have thought.

I hope you enjoy.

Heatherly Bell

A Charming Doorstep Baby

HEATHERLY BELL

HARLEQUIN
SPECIAL
EDITION

HARLEQUIN®
SPECIAL
EDITION™

Recycling programs for this product may not exist in your area.

ISBN-13: 978-1-335-59423-5

A Charming Doorstep Baby

Copyright © 2023 by Heatherly Bell

Harlequin Enterprises ULC
22 Adelaide St. West, 41st Floor
Toronto, Ontario M5H 4E3, Canada
www.Harlequin.com

Printed in U.S.A.

Bestselling author **Heatherly Bell** was born in Tuscaloosa, Alabama, but lost her accent by the time she was two. After leaving Alabama, Heatherly lived with her family in Puerto Rico and Maryland before being transplanted kicking and screaming to California's Bay Area. She now loves it here, she swears. Except the traffic.

Books by Heatherly Bell

Harlequin Special Edition

Charming, Texas

Winning Mr. Charming
The Charming Checklist
A Charming Christmas Arrangement
A Charming Single Dad

The Fortunes of Texas: Hitting the Jackpot

Winning Her Fortune

Montana Mavericks:
The Real Cowboys of Bronco Heights

Grand-Prize Cowboy

Wildfire Ridge

More than One Night
Reluctant Hometown Hero
The Right Moment

Visit the Author Profile page
at Harlequin.com for more titles.

This book is dedicated to the teachers, social workers and child advocates who work tirelessly to help children. You are the unsung heroes. Thank you for all you do.

Chapter One

"Another drink for Maribel."

Maribel Del Toro held up her palm. "No, *thanks*. I might not be driving, but I have to worry about walking while under the influence."

For an establishment that was a historical landmark, the Salty Dog Bar & Grill had mastered the art of a modern twist. The ambience fell somewhere between contemporary and classic, with a long bar of gleaming dark wood, one redbrick wall and exposed ceiling beams. Separate and on the opposite side of the bar the restaurant section was filled with booths. To top it all off, a quaint sense of small coastal town community infused the bar. Maribel loved it here.

Her brother, Max, was the occasional bartender and full-time owner. Situated on the boardwalk in the quiet town of Charming, Texas, it was the kind of place where everybody knew your name.

Especially if you were the younger sister of one of the three former Navy SEALs who owned and operated the establishment.

"You had one beer. Even I think you're skilled enough to make it to the cottages without falling." Max grinned and wiped the bar.

"Ha ha. My brother, the comedian. I'll have a soda, please and thank you."

Afterward, she'd take a leisurely walk down to her beach rental a short mile from the boardwalk. Lately, she'd been digging her toes in the sand and simply staring off into the large gulf. Her father had once said if she ever got too big for her britches, she should consider the vastness of the ocean. She often had from her childhood home in Watsonville, California. The Pacific Ocean was an entirely different feel from the Gulf Coast, but both reminded her of how small her own problems were in comparison.

The doors to the restaurant swung open and some of the customers called out.

"Val! Hey, girl."

"When are you gettin' yourself back to work?"

"Soon as my husband lets me! Believe me, I miss y'all, especially your tips." Valerie Kinsella stopped to chat with customers and let a few of them check out the bundle in her front-loaded baby carrier.

She sidled up to the bar, her hand protectively cradled on her son's head of espresso brown curls that matched his mother's. "Hey, y'all. How's it goin'?"

"Hey there." Max hooked his thumb in the direction of the back office. "If you want Cole, he's in the back checking the books. We want to give the staff a nice bonus around the holidays."

"Well, dang it, I'm going to miss out on that, too. But I didn't just come by to see Cole. I sleep next to him every night." Valerie elbowed Maribel. "How are you enjoying your vacation?"

"Loving it. The beach rental unit is just perfect."

"And even if it is hurricane season, the weather seems to be cooperating."

Oh yeah. By the way, somebody should have told Maribel. When she'd eagerly booked this vacation for November, everyone forgot to mention the tail end of hurricane season. But this part of the Gulf Coast hadn't been hit in many years, so it was considered safe. Or as safe as Mother Nature could be. In any case, the lovely row of cottages near the beach were being sold to an investor, according to her sister-in-law, Ava, and this might be Maribel's last chance to stay there.

She nodded to Valerie's baby. "What a cutie. Congratulations again."

"Wade is such a sweet baby. We're lucky." Valerie kissed the top of his head.

He was a healthy-looking kid, too, with bright blue curious eyes the same intense shade as his father's. Maribel didn't have any children of her own, but she had plenty of experience. Loads. More than she'd ever wanted, thank you. In a way, that was why she was here in Charming, taking a sabbatical from all the suffering and gnashing of teeth. It went along with her profession like the ocean to the grains of sand.

"When do you go back to teaching?" Maribel gently touched Wade's little pert nose.

"Not until after the holidays. I've had a nice maternity leave, but it's time to get back to my other kids. The students claim to miss me. I have enough cards and drawings to make me almost believe it."

Maribel spent a few more minutes being treated to Valerie's "warrior story," i.e., her labor and delivery. She was a champ, according to Cole. Valerie claimed not to remember much, which to Maribel sounded like a blessing in disguise. Mucus plug. Episiotomy. Yikes. Maribel had reached her TMI limit when Cole, the former SEAL turned golden surfer boy, came blustering out of the back office looking every bit the harried father of one.

"Hey, baby." He slid his arm around Valerie, circling it around mother and child.

Maribel had known Cole for years since he'd been a part of the brotherhood who for so long had ruled Max's life. She imagined Max and his wife would be headed to Baby Town soon, as well. And though it was information still being held private, Jordan and Rafe were newly pregnant. Maribel had been given the news by a thrilled Jordan just last week.

Maribel slid off the stool. "Well, folks, I'm going to head on back to my little beach shack now."

Shack wasn't quite the right word. She'd been pleasantly surprised to find a suite similar to resort hotel villas. It contained a separate seating area and flat-screen, attached kitchenette and separate bedroom with a second flat-screen and a king-size bed. The bedroom had sliders opening up to a small patio that led to the private beach.

"Need a ride?" Cole asked.

"Nah. Part of the ambience of Charming can only be enjoyed by strolling."

Max gave a quick wave. "Don't forget, Ava wants you over for dinner soon."

"I'm here two weeks. Plenty of time." She slid a pleading look Valerie's way. "I'm hopeful for another invite to the lighthouse, too."

"Anytime!" Cole and Valerie both said at once, making everyone laugh.

Max rolled his eyes, but he should talk. He and Ava often finished each other's sentences.

Outside, the early November evening greeted her with a mild and light wind. Summers in the gulf had resembled a sauna in every way, but autumn had so far turned out to be picture perfect. Except for the whole hurricane season thing. Still, it was warm enough during the day for trips to the beach. When she dipped her toes in, the gulf waters were less like a hot tub and more like a warm bath. Maribel ambled along the seawall, away from the boardwalk side filled with carnival-style rides for children. The succulent scent of freshly popped kettle corn and waffle cones hung thickly in the air. She passed by shops, both the Lazy Mazy kettle corn and the saltwater taffy store. The wheels of an old-fashioned machine in front of the shop's window rolled and pulled the taffy and entertained passersby. In the distance, Maribel spotted a group of surfers.

The views were everything one would expect from a bucolic beach town with a converted lighthouse, piers, docks and sea jetties. The first time she'd been here was for Max and Ava's wedding six months ago, and she'd fallen in love with the area. It was the only place she'd considered escaping when she'd decided to resign from her position as a social worker. The offer from a multi-author doctor corporation was one she'd consider while here. They wanted a psychologist on board to assist with their heavy caseload, and that meant Maribel would put her hard-earned PhD to use. Although she wasn't excited by the prospect. Maybe after this vacation, she'd be able to clear the decks and finally make a firm decision. The offer was attractive, but it would be a huge change for her. She wasn't sure she'd be able to do much good and felt at a crossroads in her life. And this was the perfect location to decide what she'd do for the rest of her professional life.

The small row of beachfront cottages were rented year-round by both residents and tourists. Maribel had lucked into a rental during the off-season, meaning she had the peace and quiet she craved. As far as she could tell so far, she had only one neighbor, immediately next door. He was the most irritating male she'd ever had the misfortune of meeting. Sort of. There was, in fact, quite a list. He was, at the moment, in the top five.

On the day she'd arrived, she'd been to the store to stock up on groceries for all the cooking she'd planned to do. Hauling no less than four paper bags inside, she'd set one down just outside the heavy front door, propping it open.

When she'd returned for it, a huge cowboy stood outside her door holding it.

"Forgot something." He'd brushed by her, striding inside like he owned the place.

"Hey," she muttered, following him.

The man spoke in a thick Texan drawl, and he hadn't said the words in a helpful way. More like an accusatory tone, as in "You dingbat, here's your bag. If you need any other help getting through life, let me know."

She'd caught him looking around the inside of her rental as if apprising its contents. But he didn't *look* like a burglar.

"I didn't forget." Maribel snatched the shopping bag from him, deciding in that moment he'd made it to the top five. Of all the nerve. She hadn't been gone a full minute.

"You might not want to just leave anything out here unattended. Unless you want someone to steal it."

Steal? Here in the small town of Charming, Texas?

She flushed at the remark. "I don't think anyone is going to steal my box of cereal or fresh fruit."

"Regardless, you should care for your property. Don't invite trouble."

Okay, so he'd figured out she was a single woman and wanted to look out for her.

"Great. If you're done with your mansplaining, I'm going to cook dinner."

"Are you liking this unit well enough? Everything in working condition?"

Now, he sounded like the landlord. *Good grief.* Top three most irritating men, easily.

"Yes, thank you, I have located everything I need." She rolled her eyes.

"I'm next door if you need anything else."

"I won't."

He'd tipped his hat, but she'd shut the door on him before he could say another word.

Since that day, she saw little of him, and that was fine with her.

Twenty minutes of an invigorating walk later, she arrived at her cottage. There was her neighbor again, the surly surfing cowboy, coming up from their lane to the beach carrying a surfboard under his arm. He might be irritating as hell, but he looked like he'd emerged from the sea shirtless, ready to sell viewers the latest popular male cologne.

She wondered whether he was attempting to cover two hero stereotypes at once. He wore a straw cowboy hat, and though this was Texas, after all, the hat didn't *quite* match with the bare chest and wet board shorts he wore low on his hips. A towel slung around his neck completed the outfit of the salty guy who once more simply nodded in her direction. Before she could say, "Howdy, neighbor," he stared straight ahead like she no longer existed.

No worries. She hadn't come here to make friends. Even if he resembled a Greek god. Thor, to be more specific—who wasn't actually from Greek mythology. This demigod had taut golden skin, a square jaw and a sensual mouth. His abs, legs and arms were chiseled to near perfection. But she was going to ignore all this because it didn't fit into her plans.

Focus. Men were not part of the plan. Even sexy irritating males, her weakness. She was here to unplug and had turned off her cell, giving her family the landline for emergencies. In her plan for mindfulness and peace, she was practicing yoga every morning before sunrise. And reading. Not from her e-reader but actual print she had to hold in her hands.

Rather than dwelling on her problems, Maribel would set them aside for now. Since months of dwelling on her problems hadn't given any answers, she was trying this new approach.

Once she'd spent enough time away from her situation, her mind would produce fresh results and ideas.

Because she had to decide soon how she would spend the rest of her life.

Dean Hunter hopped out of the shower and wrapped a towel around himself. Another day completed in his attempts to hit the waves and master the fine art of surfing. All he had to show for it? Two more fresh cuts, five new bruises and a sore knee. He had to face facts: he was a disaster on the water, having spent most of his life on a working cattle ranch. He'd been bucked off many a horse, and how interesting to find it wasn't any less pleasant to slam into the water than the ground. Seemed like water should give a little, and of course it did, more than the ground ever would. Still hurt, though, equal to the velocity with which a person slammed into a wave.

Why am I here?

A question he asked himself twice a day.

He should have simply backed out of this vacation and lost his deposit. This time was to have been a getaway with Amanda, where he'd get down on bended knee and pop the question. The cottages were going to be a surprise wedding gift to her. A way to show her all he'd accomplished. They'd have a vacation home every summer, a whole row of them. He was a damn idiot thinking that maybe he'd finally found the right woman. He and Amanda were both part of the circuit and had been for years. They had a great deal in common, and eventually they'd decided moving out of the friend zone made sense.

Then, six months ago, he'd walked in on Amanda showing Anton "The Kid" Robbins the ropes. And by "the ropes," he meant he'd walked in on her and the twenty-six-year-old, Amanda straddling him like a bucking horse. No way a man could ever unsee that. He'd walked out of his own house and moved into a hotel room. One more race to win, he'd told himself, and maybe then he'd go out on top. But that hadn't happened.

To think that Anton had been his protégé. Dean hadn't been ready to retire, but he saw the sense in training the new kids, giving them a hand up. Someone had done this for him, and he would return the favor. He couldn't ride forever, but he'd thought he would have had a little more time. Now Dean was the old guard and Anton the new. He didn't have as many injuries (yet) as Dean and was also ten years younger.

Dean still had no idea how he'd gotten it all so wrong. He hadn't been able to clearly see what had been in front of him all along. His manager had warned him about Amanda, who was beautiful but calculating. Dean had wanted to believe he'd finally found someone who would stick by him when he quit the rodeo. He'd had about six months with her, during which time she convinced him he'd found the right woman. *Yeah, not so much.*

Their breakup happened right before his last ride. He'd already been reeling when he'd taken the last blow, this one to his career. In some ways, he was still trying to get up from the last kick to his ego. At thirty-six, battered and bruised, he'd been turned in for a newer model. Anton still had plenty of mileage left on him, time to make his millions before a body part gave out on him.

So Dean should have let the opportunity to buy this investment property go. There were ten cottages, and in anticipation of his stay here to check them out thoroughly, they'd kept them vacant for him. All except Cute Stuck-up Girl next door. The moment he'd noticed he wasn't here alone as expected, he'd phoned the real estate agent.

"Thought I was going to be here by myself."

"You were, but Maribel Del Toro apparently has some influential friends in this town, friends who know the current owner and have some pull. We thought it best not to reschedule her reservation like we did the others."

"How am I supposed to inspect her unit?"

He'd already found an excuse by hurrying to help bring in a grocery bag in before she had a chance to say anything. You would have thought he'd wrecked the place instead of tried to help. He'd obviously insulted her in the process, but how else was he supposed to check inside? He never bought a dang thing before he inspected every nook and cranny, and that included a horse.

"We will give you a clause to back out if something is wrong in that unit. These deals fall apart all the time."

"And why is she right *next* to my unit?"

The real estate agent sighed. "Remember, you asked for new storm windows if you were even to consider buying. Progress on the others was not complete, and hers was the only unit available when she arrived."

By nature, Dean was a suspicious sort, and he couldn't help but wonder why these units were going far too cheaply for ocean-front property. But as a kid who'd grown up in Corpus Christi to a single mother who never had much, it would be a nice "full circle" gesture to buy this. And after years of punishing his body and garnering one buckle after another, he was a wealthy man. Still, he didn't like anyone to know it, least of all women. So he dressed like a cowboy even if he was technically a multimillionaire. At his core, he was a cowboy and always would be.

While the injury was said to be career ending, he could have gone through rehab and come back stronger than ever. Having come from nothing, he'd been wise about his investments, and while others enjoyed buckle bunnies, gambling and drinking, Dean had socked away every nickel. He had investments all over Texas, including his ranch in Hill Country.

In the end, he'd forced himself to walk away from the rodeo before he didn't have a body left to enjoy the other pleasantries in life. Oh yeah. That was why he was here in Charming trying his hand at surfing in the Gulf of Mexico during hurricane season. It was just the shot of adrenaline a junkie like him needed.

He would find his footing in his new world with zero illusions he'd find a second career as a competitive surfer. Instead, it was time for the second part of his life to begin, the part that was supposed to matter.

Life *after* the rodeo. Life after poverty.

He'd already been coming here for a short time every summer just to remember his roots. He'd drive from Corpus Christi to Charming, counting his blessings. Enjoying the coastal weather.

Remembering his mother.

Once, he could recall having ambitions that went beyond the rodeo. An idea and a plan to fix for others what had been broken in his own life. Somewhere along the line, he'd forgotten every last one of those dreams. He was here to hopefully remember some of them in the peace and quiet of this small town. Here, no one would disturb him. No one except his feisty neighbor, that is, who behaved as if he'd deeply insulted her by carrying in her groceries. She'd immediately put him on the defensive, seeing as it had merely been an excuse to get inside her unit. It was as if she could read his mind. He didn't like it.

He often watched Cute Stuck-up Girl from a distance as she sank her feet in the sand and read a book. Two days ago, he'd seen her fighting the beach umbrella she'd been setting up for shade. It was almost bigger than her, which was part of the problem. She'd cursed and carried on until Dean was two seconds away from offering his help. He'd walk over there and issue instructions on how to put the umbrella up until she got all red in the face again with outrage. The thought made him chuckle. He'd put the umbrella up *for* her if she'd let him. Not likely.

Finally, she got it to stay up and did a little victory dance when she must have assumed no one was watching.

And he'd found a laugh for the first time in months.

After changing clothes and towel-drying his hair, Dean plopped on his favorite black Stetson and headed to the local watering hole. A little place along the boardwalk that he'd discovered a few years ago sandwiched between other storefronts and gift shops. At the Salty Dog Bar & Grill, the occasional bartender and owner there was a surfer who'd given Dean plenty of tips. Cole Kinsella had even offered Dean one of his older boards, since as a new father, he wasn't taking to the water as often.

Safe to say, Dean liked the bar and the people in it from the moment he'd strode inside and momentarily indulged in one of his favorite fantasies: buying a sports bar. It was one of the few investments he didn't have because he'd been talked out of it too many times to count. This place resembled a sports bar, but was more of a family place that also happened to have a bar. The restaurant section sat next to the bar separated only by the booths. Instead of huge flat-screens on every spare amount of space, there were chalkboards with the specials written out in fancy white cursive.

Everyone was friendly and welcoming. The first night Dean had come in, he'd met a group of senior citizens who were having some kind of a poetry meeting.

The only gentleman in the group, Roy Finch, had offered to buy Dean a beer.

"Don't mind if I do." Dean nodded. "Thank you, sir."

"You're a cowboy?"

"Yes, sir. Born and bred." Dean tipped his hat.

"Don't usually see that many of you here on the gulf."

"Our profession usually keeps us far from the coast."

"What you doin' in these parts?"

"Good question." Dean took a pull of the beer the bartender had set in front of him. "I guess I'm lookin' for another profession."

"All washed out?"

"That obvious?" Dean snorted. "I was part of the rodeo circuit longer than I care to say."

"Thought I recognized you. Tough life."

They'd discussed the rodeo and the current front

runners, which unfortunately included Anton. The man thought he was God's gift to women, overindulging in buckle bunnies and earning himself quite a reputation both on and off the circuit.

Dean had gone over a few of his injuries with Roy, but held back on the worst ones. Mr. Finch had introduced him to his fiancée, Lois, and some other women who were with him and were all part of a group calling themselves the Almost Dead Poets Society. Every night since then, Dean met someone new.

Now, he sidled up to the bar, but the surfer dude wasn't behind it. A dark-haired guy named Max, going by what everyone called him, was taking orders.

"What can I get you?" he asked Dean in an almost-menacing tone.

"Cold beer."

"We have several IPAs, domestic and imported." He rattled off names, sounding more like a sommelier than a bartender.

"Domestic, thanks."

"Here you go," he said a moment later, uncapping a bottle and taking Dean's cash.

This guy wasn't quite as chatty and friendly as Cole had been. He was also busy as the night wore on and, after a while, got grumpy.

"Max," someone called out. "C'mon! I ordered a mojito about an *hour* ago."

This was a great exaggeration, as Dean had listened to the man order it no more than fifteen minutes ago.

"And if you ask me again, you're not getting it *tonight*."

Dean would go out on a limb and guess this man was one of the owners of the bar. Cole had explained they were three former Navy SEALs who had retired and saved the floundering bar from foreclosure.

Turning his back to the bar, Dean spread his arms out and took in the sights. A busy place, the waitresses in the adjacent dining area flitted from one table to the next. He saw couples, families and a group of younger women taking up an entire table.

"Hey there, cowboy," a soft sweet voice to his right said. "I'm Twyla."

Dean immediately zeroed in on the source, a beautiful brunette who looked to be quite a bit younger than him. He shouldn't let that bother him, but for reasons he didn't understand, only younger women hit on him. He guessed it to be the fascination with the cowboy archetype, which usually happened when traveling in urban cities or coastal areas. He happened to know men who'd had nothing to do with ranches or rodeos who wore Western boots, a straw hat and ambled into a bar. They never left alone.

But a beautiful woman would only take time and attention away from Dean's surfing. Besides, were he to take up with any woman, it would be with the girl next door. Literally. She was as gorgeous a woman as he'd ever laid eyes on. Dark hair that fell in waves around her shoulders, chocolate brown eyes that made a man feel…seen.

"Dean. It's a pleasure." He nodded, failing to give her a last name. She didn't seem like the type to follow the rodeo, but one never knew.

He intended to remain anonymous while in Charming, though a few had already recognized him. The night before, he'd given out his autograph and taken a few photos with a family visiting from Hill Country. He ought to ditch the hat and shoot for a little less obvious.

"You're on vacation?" Twyla asked.

"How did you guess?"

"Not many cowboy types around here."

"Actually, I'm a surfer."

Speaking of exaggerations…

"You're kidding. Well, you're in the right place. Pretty soon the waves are going to kick up, depending on whether a system hits us. But don't worry, we haven't had a direct hit in decades." She offered her hand. "I own the bookstore in town, Once Upon a Book."

Her hand was soft and sweet, making Dean recall just how long it had been since he'd been with a woman. *Too* long. And even though it seemed like bookstores had become as out-of-date and useless as broken-down cowboys like him, he didn't feel a need to connect with this woman.

She had a look about her he recognized too well: she had a *thing* about cowboys. He wasn't interested in indulging in those fantasies. Been there, done that, bought the saddle. He was done with women who were interested in the part of him he was leaving behind. Rodeo had been fun, his entire life for two decades.

And now it was over.

They chatted a few more minutes about nothing in particular, and then Dean set his bottle down on the bar, deciding to call it an early night.

"Nice meeting ya."

"I'll see you around?" she asked.

"You will." He waved and strode outside.

The sun was nearing the end of its slow slide down the horizon, sinking into the sea, assuring him the sky would be dark by the time he drove to his rental. He looked forward to another night of peace and quiet, retiring to bed alone and hogging the damn covers. There were good parts of being alone, few that they were, and he needed to remember them lest he be tempted to remedy the situation.

He arrived to find a basket in front of Cute Stuck-up Girl's house she'd obviously forgotten to bring inside, again, and Dean figured he'd knock on the door and finally introduce himself. This time, he wouldn't be as irritated and try on a smile or two. Maybe even apologize for their rough beginning.

Just a quick hello, and he'd be home lickety-split. He stepped over the crushed shell walkway between them, heading toward the front door.

Then the basket made a tiny mewing sound.

What the hell?

Dean approached and bent low to view, with utter horror, that his neighbor had left her baby on the doorstep.

Chapter Two

Maribel was in the middle of chopping onions for her mother's arroz con pollo recipe when she heard a loud pounding on the front door. This was odd, because everyone she knew in Charming would call or text first. But she'd told Ava to drop by anytime. Maribel dried her hands on a dish towel, then walked toward the door. The pounding had become so fierce it could not possibly be her sweet sister-in-law. This was more like a man's fist. Or a hammer.

There was urgency in the knocking. She could feel it, like a pounding deep in her gut. With an all too familiar deep sense of flight-or-fight syndrome coursing through her, she swung the door open.

There stood her neighbor, holding a large basket.

His expression was positively murderous. "Forget something?"

Wondering why he was still so concerned about her forgetting stuff and ready to tell him off, she peered inside the basket. "Oh, you have a baby."

"Your baby." He snarled, then pushed his way inside, setting the basket down.

"*Excuse* me?"

"It was right on your doorstep. This is dangerous. How absent-minded are you, exactly? Are you going to tell me you didn't even realize?"

Her hackles went up immediately at even the suggestion that she, of all people, would forget a *baby*. He didn't know her or her history. He quickly went from top five to number one most irritating male she'd ever met.

"Number one!" she shouted.

"*Excuse* me?"

"I don't have a baby, *sir*!"

"Well, it's not *my* baby!"

They stared daggers at each other for several long beats. His eyes were an interesting shade of amber, and at the moment, they were dark with hostility. Aimed at her, of all people. Because he didn't know her and that she'd sooner be roasted over hot coals than put a child at risk.

Her mind raced. In the past few days, she'd never seen him with a baby. No sign of a woman or child next door, so her instinct was to believe him. It probably wasn't his baby. And either he was certifiably insane, or he really was indignant that she would have forgotten her baby.

Which meant... Realization dawned on Maribel and appeared to simultaneously hit him.

They both rushed out the front door, him slightly ahead of her. Maribel ran to the edge of the short path in one direction, and Cowboy went in the other.

"Hey!" he shouted after whoever would have done this terrible thing. "Hey! Get back here!"

"Do you see anyone?"

"You go back inside with the baby. I'll go see if I can find any sign of who did this." He took off at a run, jogging down the lane leading to the beach.

Her breaths were coming sharp and ragged. Maybe this was a joke. Yes, a big practical joke on Maribel Del Toro, the burned-out former social worker. But she didn't know of anyone who'd leave a baby unattended outside as a joke. It wasn't funny. Who would be this stupid and careless?

Inside, the baby lay quietly in the basket, kicking at the blanket, completely unaware of the trauma he or she had caused. Why *Maribel's* door? And who was this desperate? Almost every fire department in the country had a safe haven for dropping a baby off, no questions asked. Of course, Charming *was* small enough to only have a volunteer fire department, and she wasn't sure they even had a station in town. But Houston was only thirty minutes away and had a large hospital and fire department.

Dressed in pink and surrounded by pink and white

blankets, a small stack of diapers was shoved to one side of the basket. The baby looked to be well cared for. Two cans of formula and a bottle were on the other side. Obviously, a very deliberate, premeditated attempt to get rid of a baby. Maribel unwrapped the child from the soft blanket and unbuttoned the sleeper. As she'd suspected, due to the baby's size, she found no signs of a healing umbilical cord. Not a newborn. The belly button had completely healed. Maribel's educated guess would make the infant around two to three months old.

Someone had lovingly cared for this baby for months and then given up. Why?

The question should be: Why this time?

Drugs? Alcohol? Homelessness? An abusive home? For years, Maribel had witnessed situations in which both children and infants had to be removed from a home. Usually, the need became apparent at first sight. Garbage inside the home, including drug paraphernalia. Empty alcohol bottles. Both kids and babies in dirty clothes and overflowing diapers. No proper bed for the child or food.

But she'd never seen a baby this well cared for left behind.

"Where's your mommy?" Maribel mused as she checked the baby out from head to toe.

A few minutes later, Cowboy came bursting through Maribel's front door slightly out of breath.

"I couldn't find anyone."

"I don't understand this. Why leave the baby at

my front door?" Then a thought occurred out of the blue, and she pointed to him. "Hang on. What if they meant to leave the baby at *your* front door but got the wrong house?"

"Mine?" He tapped his chest. "Why *my* house?"

"Let's see. What are the odds somewhere along the line you impregnated a woman? Maybe she's tired and wants *you* to take a turn with your child."

Even as she said the words, Maribel recognized the unfairness behind them. She'd made a rash conclusion someone this attractive had to be a player with a ton of women in his past. And also, apparently, someone who didn't practice safe sex.

And from the narrowed eyes and tight jawline, he'd taken this as a dig.

"That's insulting. I don't have any children. If I had a baby, believe me, I'd *know* about it."

"It doesn't always work that way, Cowboy." She picked up the baby and held her close, rubbing her back in slow and even strokes.

"My name's *Dean*, not Cowboy." He pointed to the diapers. "What's that?"

"Diapers," Maribel deadpanned. "Are you not acquainted with them?"

"This." He bent low and, from between the diapers, picked out a sheet of paper.

"What is it?" Maribel said.

Dean unfolded and read. As he did, his face seemed to change colors. He went from golden boy to gray boy.

He lowered the note, then handed it to Maribel. "It's not signed."

Maribel set the baby in the basket, then read:

Her name is Brianna, and she's a really good baby. Sometimes she even sleeps through the night. The past three months have been hard, but I want to keep my baby. I just need a couple of weeks to figure some things out. Please take care of her until I come back. Tell her mommy will miss her, but I promise I'm coming back. I left some formula and diapers, and I promise to pay you back for any more you have to buy. She likes it when I sing to her.

"Figure a few things out" could mean anything from drug addiction to a runaway teen.

And this troubled girl had left the baby…with Maribel.

"I swear, I… I don't know who would have done this. I don't even live in Charming. I'm here on vacation."

"She must know you somehow. More importantly, she trusts you with her baby."

"She's trusted the wrong person if she thinks I'm going to allow this to happen."

He narrowed his eyes. "What does that mean?"

"We have to call the police."

"No. We *don't*."

"Just one week ago, I was an employed social

worker with the state of California. I know about these things."

"Sounds like you're no longer employed, and we're in the state of Texas, last I checked."

"That doesn't change facts. This is child abandonment, pure and simple."

"Except it's *not*." He snapped the letter out of Maribel's hands and tapped on the writing. "It's clearly written here that she'll be back. She's asked you to babysit. That's *all*."

"Are you kidding me? She left the baby on my *doorstep*. Babysitting usually involves *asking* someone first. An exchange of information. Anything could have happened to her baby. You were upset when I left a bag of *groceries* on the doorstep."

"Is it possible she rang the doorbell, and you didn't hear? You took your sweet time coming to the door for me, and I was about to knock it down."

"It's…possible." She shook her head. "I don't know. We should call the cops. At the very least, get her checked out at the hospital and make sure she's okay."

"No. If we take her to a hospital, too many questions will be asked."

"Those questions *need* to be asked! We don't know what we're dealing with here."

"We know *exactly* what we're dealing with here, thanks to the note. A probably young and overwhelmed single mom is asking you to babysit. You're the one person who could stand between her ability to ever see her baby again."

You're the one person who could stand between her ability to ever see her baby again.

His words hit her with sharp slings and a force he might have not intended. They felt personal, slamming into her, slicing her in two.

"Nice try. But I refuse to be guilt-tripped into abandoning my principles."

He snorted. "Principles. That's funny."

"What's funny about principles? Don't you have them?"

"Principles won't work if there's no real intent behind them. Or is family reunification a myth?"

She crossed her arms. Interesting. Her analytical brain took this tip and filed it away for future use. The man seemed to know a few things about the system.

"Of course it's not a myth. It's the goal, but too many times, the parents are unable to meet their part of the deal. The children come first. Always."

"And the children want to be with their parents. It's the number one truth universally acknowledged. If you call law enforcement, that's going to complicate everything."

"That will simply start the clock ticking, and she'll have forty-eight hours to return."

"I can't let you do that. This mother clearly wants her baby back."

Everything inside Maribel tensed when this total stranger told her what she could and couldn't do. He didn't know how many times she'd had faith in a parent, worked for their reunification, only to be burned time and again. The last time had nearly ruined her. She was done rescuing people.

"I can't… I can't take her."

"You're choosing not to. Do me a favor? Stay out of this. I'll take the baby."

"*You* will. You?"

For reasons she didn't quite understand, the surfing cowboy had strong feelings about this. And she got it. A baby in need brought out universal emotions. She wanted to help, but the right thing to do was to call the authorities. Eventually, if the mother *proved* herself to be worthy, she'd get her baby back through the proper channels. Parents should prove they were capable of caring for their children. That way, all could be reassured this wasn't simply a temporary lapse in the girl's judgment. Everyone could be certain the baby was returned to a safe environment.

Dean took the baby from Maribel, then bent to pick up the baby's basket. He moved toward the front door. "Don't let us bother you."

"Wait a second here. What do *you* know about babies? Have you ever had children?"

"No, but I know enough. The rest I'll learn online."

"Online? So, you're going to *google* it?"

"Listen, there are YouTube videos on everything. I guarantee you I can figure this out. You don't need a PhD to change a diaper."

Her neck jerked back. It was unnerving the way he seemed to read her, to know her, before she'd told him a thing. No, you didn't need a *PhD* to change a diaper, but to understand why people reacted in the ways they did. To meet them in their dysfunction and try to help. The problem was all bets were off when addiction was part of the picture. Then parents didn't behave logically. They made decisions not even in their *own* best interest, let alone a child's. And Maribel didn't know whether this mother was an addict who could no longer care for her child. She didn't know anything at all about this mother, and the thought filled her with anxiety.

She cocked her head and went for logic. "This is going to interfere with your precious surfing time, you know."

She'd noticed him on the beach with his board every day, like it was his religion.

"Not a problem." He turned to her as though giving her one more chance to reconsider. "But if that's an offer to babysit a time or two, I'd take you up on it."

"Babysit? For all practical purposes, that's *my baby* you're holding. She left her for me to take care of."

"And you've said you can't violate your principles, so…"

"I also don't know whether I can trust you to watch YouTube videos and figure out how to take care of a baby."

"Well, damn. Looks like your principles are in conflict with one another."

Really? Tell me about it!

Not long ago, this had been her life. A desire to help but forced to follow rules set in place with the best of intentions. Foster care was never the horrible place pop culture and the news media led people to believe. It was only meant to be a temporary and safe home. Too many negative stories made the press, and did not acknowledge those angelic foster parents who cared for children with what amounted to a pittance of a salary.

"While you cuddle up with your principles tonight, I'll be next door with Brianna." Then he left with the baby.

"Number one!" she shouted behind him, but either he hadn't heard or decided not to acknowledge it.

She wasn't cuddling up to her principles, she was *living* with them. Doing the right thing. And yet… procedure would involve alerting the police. The problem was she seemed to be in a gray area, but ethics were always important, regardless of whether legalities were involved.

You're here to unplug. Mindfulness is the key. You're going to teach yourself to cook. Read feel-good fiction. Stay off your cell, all social media and recharge. You have a major decision to make.

Last month, an old headhunter friend had approached and offered Maribel a position with a six-figure salary. She'd be taking over the caseload of a therapist who had counseled the children of the Silicon Valley elite. Anxiety, depression and ADHD were core issues. Maribel had a knee-jerk reaction to the proposition: no. But maybe she could do some good there. It would be something so different from what she'd been doing for years. A chance to use her education and experience in a different way.

She only had a few more weeks to decide before they looked for someone else.

Maribel went back to her dinner of arroz con pollo, so rudely interrupted by both her neighbor and a baby. As she opened cans of tomato sauce and stirred them into the rice, she relaxed and unwound. Her breathing returned to normal, and her shoulders unkinked. Routines were good to employ in the aftermath of shock. They soothed. They reminded a person life would go on.

On the day Maribel discovered the toddler she'd helped reunite with his mother had been rushed to the hospital with dehydration, she'd brushed her teeth in the middle of the day. Later, she would come to doubt every decision she'd ever made, including the one to become a social worker.

Despite the fact Dean had let Maribel off the hook, she couldn't ignore the mother's request. The baby was her responsibility, and she never shirked her duties. Not from the time she was working with her parents in the strawberry fields of Watsonville to the moment of her PhD dissertation. She, Maribel Del Toro, was no quitter.

She didn't want a surfing cowboy dude who had to google *diapering* to take care of the baby. And even if Maribel had a good sense of people, she didn't know this man. She'd let him take a baby next door, where he might hopelessly bungle it all. In all good conscience, she couldn't just stand by.

Ten minutes later, she turned off the stove and banged on the door to *his* cottage.

He opened the door, almost as if he'd expected her. But then he walked toward the connected bedroom with barely a glance, simply leaving it for her to choose to walk inside or not.

"I can't walk away from her. It's my responsibility," she said.

Since he didn't say a word, she closed the front door and followed him past the sitting room area, the kitchenette and into the bedroom. He'd emptied a dresser drawer and placed Brianna in it, surrounded by her blankets.

"This is a temporary bed for her." He ran a hand through his hair, looking more than a little out of sorts. "Maybe I should buy a crib."

He'd removed the hat, and she wasn't surprised to find golden locks of hair had been under it, curling at his neck and almost long enough to be put in a short ponytail.

Hands in the pockets of his jeans, he lowered his head to study the baby as if mulling over a complicated algebra word problem.

Brianna cooed and gave him a drooly smile. Aw, she was such a cute baby. Beautiful dark eyes and curls of black hair. Her beautiful skin was a light brown. She could be African American, Latina or multiracial.

"As you said, babysitting her is temporary. You don't need to invest in a crib. Maybe this, um, drawer will do for now."

"You *approve*?"

The corner of his lip curled up in a half smile, and something went tight in Maribel's belly. The cowboy's eyes were an interesting shade some would call hazel, others might simply call amber. But they were no longer hot with anger.

She tilted her chin and met his eyes. "Let's just say I'm in new territory here, but so far, so good."

"You're going to help me?"

"It would be irresponsible of me to let you do this on your own."

He shook his head. "Those principles in conflict again. Pesky little things."

"Don't make fun of me. This is serious."

"Yeah, it is. A baby needs you. I know what I'm going to do. What about you?"

She still didn't know, but maybe she didn't *have* to make an immediate decision. It was entirely possible the mother would be back by tomorrow at the latest, regretting what she'd done and missing her baby. Unfortunately, Maribel was too jaded to believe this a real possibility.

But she wanted to.

"We don't even know if she'll be gone the full two weeks. She could come back sooner."

"Exactly." Dean picked up a diaper. "The way I

look at this, Brianna is going to need more diapers. I already went through two of them."

"*Two?* You've been in here for fifteen minutes."

He scowled and scratched his chin. "She wet while I was changing her. Is that…normal?"

Oh boy. This guy really didn't know a thing. Then again, how often did men babysit siblings, nieces or nephews even if they had them? Not often, at least not in her family.

Dean had already explained he had no children of his own. *That he knew of.*

"It's normal. You're lucky Brianna isn't a boy. Sometimes the stream goes long and wide."

"Okay." Dean crossed his arms and gazed at her from under hooded lids. "Thanks for the four-one-one."

"Um, you're welcome." Self-consciously, Maribel pulled on the sleeve of her sundress and chewed on her lower lip.

She didn't usually wear dresses, and that might be the reason she was so ill at ease here with him. Usually she wore pantsuits, her hair up in a bun. Men were still occasionally strange creatures to her, who had ideas she didn't quite grasp.

Watching this particular man from a safe distance had been comfortable. Easy. She could ogle him all she wanted from the privacy of her own cottage and realize nothing would come of it. Now, standing next to him, there was a charge between them. He'd really *noticed* her. She suddenly felt a little…naked. And a lot…awkward.

"You mind watching her while I go buy some diapers and formula?" he said.

"Go ahead."

A perfect opportunity. While here alone, Maribel planned on surreptitiously checking out Dean's unit. It wasn't that she had trust issues, no sir, but if he was going to watch the baby *she'd* been entrusted with, she should make sure he could be relied on with any child. She wouldn't call it snooping, exactly. More like a light criminal background check.

"Be right back." He grabbed his keys.

"And don't forget baby wipes."

"Okay. Wipes."

She pointed. "*Baby* wipes. Don't get the Lysol ones."

"Speaking of mansplaining." He quirked a brow and gave her the side-eye before he walked out the door.

Snooping commenced immediately. First, she checked on Brianna, who, with a clean diaper, had gone back to snoozing. Admittedly the drawer was an ingenious and scrappy idea from a man who'd probably had to figure things out in the wilderness when all he had for supper was a stick and a rabbit.

Okay, Maribel, he's a cowboy, not Paul Bunyon.

She knew little of life on the range, where she assumed he lived. Checking through his luggage, she found plenty of shirts and jeans. Interesting. He wore dark boxer briefs. Not even white socks but dark ones. Wasn't that against cowboy regulations?

Put the underwear down and back away, Maribel.

His underwear and clothes told her nothing about the man. Importantly, she hadn't found a gun or a buck knife. She rifled through drawers in each room, finding real estate flyers and Ava's "Welcome to Charming" Chamber of Commerce handout. But nothing embarrassing, dangerous or disgusting. She checked the medicine cabinet and under the mattress for those pesky recreational drugs. On her principles, she'd whisk this baby away in a New York minute even if she found the (ahem) legal stuff. Nothing. So far, he checked out.

Then she found a pack of condoms in his nightstand drawer, and it snapped her back to reality.

What am I doing?

She sat on the bed and stared at the wall, covering her face. If only her colleagues could see her now. They'd no longer have any doubts that she'd done the right thing by resigning from the California Department of Social Services.

They'd no longer have any doubt that she'd lost all faith in humanity. She no longer believed in people. She no longer believed in second chances.

This poor man was trying to do a good thing here, and she'd found his condoms, violating his privacy in every way. None of her business. Hey, at least he was prepared. She could find nothing wrong with the man who'd offered to care for the baby, so she didn't have an excuse to call the authorities. He was right to hope. Maybe. There was a memory nagging at the edge of Maribel's mind, but she couldn't pin it down. Last week, when she'd been to the Once Upon a Book store with Stacy Cruz, Maribel might have mentioned her former career in social services. There had been a teenage girl there looking through the mystery section.

She could give this mother at least twenty-four hours.

One day to regret her decision and come running back for her baby.

The mother would be back, and if she didn't return, *then* Maribel would call the police.

Chapter Three

Dean stood in the middle of aisle fourteen, feeling like a giant idiot. He'd asked for wipes and the clerk sent him straight here, but this wasn't right. These were the Lysol cleaning wipes Maribel had warned him about, as if he didn't know any better. The clerk had simply assumed *he* didn't have a baby, but obviously must have a bathroom or a kitchen to clean. And he hadn't been specific enough. *Baby* wipes.

Maybe babysitting Brianna wasn't such a great idea. If only his pretty neighbor would have agreed to watch the baby and let him off the hook. What was wrong with her, anyway? He expected most women would want to babysit a cute baby, but then again, he'd wager she wasn't most women. It turned out she was a social worker with an inherent bias against mothers who made mistakes.

People like Maribel had changed the trajectory of Dean's life.

He wandered down the aisles and finally found the baby stuff. There were packages of diapers in all manner of sizes. Newborn, the smallest, and then differing numbered sizes by weight. He had no idea how much the baby weighed. In two seconds, he was overwhelmed. He didn't even know how old this baby was and hadn't thought to get Maribel's cell number so he could text her from the store. What *size*? He wanted to get eight to fourteen pounds because that made sense, but maybe over fourteen pounds would be best. Better to have a bigger size than too small, right? He knew that much, anyway.

The formula deal was a lot easier to figure out, so he picked up a case. The baby wipes, once he found them, also easy. Did not require a size, only choosing between scented, unscented, with added aloe vera and hypoallergenic. He chose the ones for sensitive skin, just in case.

As Dean was holding the newborn size diapers in one hand and the next larger size in the other, a man came rushing into the aisle and began snatching pacifiers off the rack like there might soon be a shortage of them. Pacifiers! Dean should have thought of that. Before the dude grabbed them all, Dean reached for one.

"Those are the best. Orthodontists recommend them," the man said, noticing Dean.

"Is there a sale going on?"

"Is there? Hope so. We're trying to wean her from these, but it's not working. And no matter what we do, we can never have enough of these on hand. We've lost so many of them under furniture, beds, cars, anywhere. I figure when we move, we're going to find a treasure trove of old and hairy pacifiers. They didn't just *disappear.* Must be hiding somewhere. It's like losing a sock in the dryer. No one has figured out where the other one goes. It's a mystery. Well, pacifiers are like clean socks."

"Uh-huh." Dean cleared his throat and examined the packaging. "How many should I get for my baby?"

"How old is she?"

"Um, she's really…*young.*"

The man quirked a brow, thankfully accepting Dean's ignorance as to the age of his pretend child.

"You look familiar. You're that beginning surfer who hangs out at the Salty Dog, aren't you? Cole told me about you."

Dean's hackles went up at being referred to as "beginning" anything, but it was an unfortunately fair assessment.

"I'm Dean Hunter. And you are…?"

He offered his hand in a firm grip. "Adam Cruz. Nice to meet you. I'm one of the Salty Dog owners."

"Pleasure." Dean tipped his hat and reframed his

story. "I'm, uh, babysitting? My niece. For my sister, she…she forgot to…"

Tell me how old her baby is?

Adam eyed the diapers Dean held. "Leave enough diapers? They go through those fast. My wife and I have a daughter, too. That's nice of you to babysit. I take people up on that every chance I get. I love my daughter, but holy cow, I need more time with my wife. Ya know?"

"Um, yeah. That's actually why I'm doing this. My sister needed some time with the wife." Dean winced, realizing he'd outed his nonexistent, invisible sister.

"And you're probably wondering what you got yourself into now."

Dean chuckled and rubbed his chin. "Ha, yeah. You could say that."

"Don't worry. I was terrified the first time I held my baby, afraid I'd break her."

"Yeah, that's how I feel."

Since the moment he'd called Maribel's bluff and hauled the baby with him next door, he had no idea what he was doing and if he'd somehow do more harm than good. Add to that the anxiety of wondering if the mother would come back as promised or if his next-door neighbor would get to be right. She would then turn him into the authorities right along with the baby.

He took the baby, she'd point and say. *And then proceeded to watch YouTube videos on how to take care*

*of her. It was a recipe for disaster from the get-go. I
tried to stop him!*

He could almost see *Rodeo Today*'s front-page
headline:

Four-Time World Champ Quits Rodeo Circuit
to Steal Someone's Baby

Dean held up the two different sizes of diapers.
"Which one?"

"Easy. Unless your baby was delivered just today
or premature, the newborn size is going to be too
small. I made the same rookie mistake. She didn't
fit into newborn by the time she was three days old.
I'd get the next one up, twelve to eighteen pounds."

"Hey, thanks, buddy. I appreciate it."

Adam waved and rushed away, taking ten pacifiers with him.

When Dean arrived back to the cottage a few minutes later, the noises from inside sounded like *ten*
angry babies in there, not *one*. Panic roiled inside
of him, but he had nowhere to run. He was going to
have to go inside and deal with this mess.

Maribel paced the floor with the screaming child.
"Oh my God, you're back! Help!"

Her face flushed and pink, her eyes were nearly
popping out of their sockets.

"What did you *do*? What's wrong with the baby?"

"You assume I did something to cause this? How

about if you don't accuse me, and I won't accuse you?"

Somehow, he expected her to be better at this, though it might be unfair of him to assume so because she had a uterus. In his case, he would have done better at delivering this child than he probably would taking care of it. It couldn't be much different than assisting in the birth of a calf. And as a bonus, baby cows didn't cry.

"Make a bottle! Quick! She could be hungry. I've already changed her. You did buy more bottles, didn't you?"

Bottles. He forgot the bottles. Stupid Adam leading him to the pacifiers like they were made of gold when Dean should have focused on more bottles instead.

"She left one in the basket. Get it! Now!"

"Stop ordering me around."

He grabbed the bottle and a can of formula, grumbling the entire time.

What had she been doing when he'd been sweating in the store aisle over diapers? All she'd had to do was watch the baby. How hard could that be? She was a sweet little angel the whole fifteen minutes she'd been in his dresser drawer. Following the directions, he mixed the powder with water and poured it into the bottle, shook it then carried it over to Maribel.

"Did you warm it?"

"I was supposed to warm it? Here, give it back. I'll use the microwave."

"Not the microwave!" She hissed. "Good lord, you don't know *anything*. Here, you take her. I'll warm the bottle."

Dean took the baby, who didn't look anything like the angelic little bundle from earlier. Now she was a wriggling mess with a wail that would kill most grown men. Her little hands were curled into fists like she was mad as hell. He swore he could see her tonsils.

"Hey, hey. Listen, I'm trying to help you. Look, I know you're mad your mama left, but that's not my fault. She'll be back. I hope."

She better come back. He was willing to give the mother the benefit of the doubt, but someone who would abandon her baby and never return was lower than dirt. He hoped she had a damn good excuse.

Dean did his best to pace, shuffle-walk and swing, imitating Maribel. Brianna stopped crying for one second when she opened her eyes, as if shocked someone else was holding her. Still clearly not the person she wanted. Her silence was a momentary lapse, as if taking a breath and gaining strength. She went right back to crying with rejuvenated energy.

"Okay." Maribel appeared with the bottle and pointed to his couch. "Already tested for temperature. Just sit down with her."

He'd never been this awkward and bumbling in his life, but did as Maribel ordered, resenting every second of her authority. Balancing Brianna in the crook of his elbow, he eased the rubber tip of the bottle into her open mouth. She sucked away at the bottle with fervor.

Maribel collapsed on the couch next to Dean. "Guess she was just hungry."

"Why didn't you feed her while I was gone?" The mother had left one can of formula and a bottle after all.

"Are you *kidding* me? You don't know how hard this is! I couldn't hold her and make the formula. I only have two hands, and she cried louder every time I put her down."

More and more, Dean worried he couldn't do this on his own. And she obviously couldn't, either.

"Are all babies this *loud*?"

"She has a good set of lungs on her. I thought she'd never stop." She leaned back. "Oh, would you listen to that?"

"What?"

"Silence. I never knew how much I loved it until it was gone."

He eyed Maribel with suspicion. "How long has she been crying? She was fine before I left."

"She just took one look at me and started wailing. It's hard not to take it personally." Maribel leaned forward, watching the baby take the bottle.

This put Maribel at his elbow, dark hair so close to him he could smell the coconut sweet flowery scent. Cute Stuck-up Girl smelled incredible. His irritation with her ebbed.

"Aw, she's so cute. Check out her perfect skin." She caressed the baby's cheek with the back of her hand.

If it could be said they were staring at the baby, which they probably were, she stared right back. Her dark eyes were wide as she took them both in. This was one smart baby, alert and aware *something* had changed.

"Thanks for helping me," Dean finally said. "I'm sorry if I sound grumpy. Obviously, I couldn't have done this without you."

"I saw how strongly you felt about this."

"I'd say we both have equally strong feelings."

She sighed and offered Brianna her finger, and the little hand fisted around it. "It's just… I've seen this kind of thing before too many times, and it doesn't end well."

"Never?"

Dean didn't want to hear this. He wanted to believe the mother would return. Sometimes all a mother needed was for someone to have a little faith in her.

Sometimes that's all anyone needed.

"Not with abandoned babies. There's generally abuse in the home, a teenager trying to hide the unwanted pregnancy." She shook her head. "You don't want to hear the rest."

Dean swallowed hard. "But did anyone ever leave a note saying they'd be back for her baby?"

To Dean, the note the mother had left was filled with hope. He remembered too well the taste of hope. No one should be denied a second chance.

"Not to my knowledge."

"Then it's possible. You just haven't heard of any instances. Granted, I agree this is unusual."

"I want to believe she'll come back, but there have been too many disappointments along the line for me. Addiction is powerful. It overcomes love."

That was one belief Dean would never accept. Not in his lifetime.

"Sorry, no. Nothing can overcome love."

Maribel turned her gaze from the baby to him, forcing him to realize how close she was. She had a full mouth and deep brown eyes that shimmered with the hint of a smile. Damn, she was…breathtaking. Much better-looking close up. He'd noticed her, of course, on the beach wearing a skimpy red bikini, displaying long legs and a heart-shaped behind. They often passed each other: her sitting under the umbrella reading, him coming back from his surfing day. After their disastrous first meeting, she'd been easier to dismiss from a safe distance with a curt nod. Far easier than to remind himself he didn't need or want any complications like the type a beautiful woman would bring into his life.

Get your act together before you even think to ask someone to tag along.

Her lips quirked in the start of a smile. "That's… certainly not what I expected you to say."

"Why? You think cowboys don't believe in love?"

"Honestly, you'll have to forgive me because I'm

not sure most *men* believe in love. Or at least, I'm not meeting them."

"Not sure who you've been dating, but that's a pretty sad statement."

"It is, isn't it?" Maribel leaned back, putting some distance between them, as if only now aware of how close she'd been. "I'm sorry to make such a blanket statement. You're right, there are some men who believe in love."

"But these are not the men you're dating. Why not?"

"Well, it's not like they wear a sign."

He snorted. "They don't wear a sign, but there are *signs*."

She simply stared at him for a moment as if she was still trying to decide whether or not he could be trusted.

"What are we going to do tonight?" She nudged her chin to Brianna. "About her?"

"We? I'll let her sleep in the drawer, or maybe I'll just lay her on the bed next to me."

She narrowed her eyes like she thought maybe this was a bad idea. "Are you a light or heavy sleeper?"

"Light." And lately, he hadn't been sleeping at all. But that was a story for another day. "It's a big bed. I won't roll over on her."

Maribel stood. "Okay. You take the first night, and tomorrow I'll take the second."

"You trust me? What if I'm some weirdo?"

"Some weirdo who wants to take care of a baby

so her mother won't lose custody? I guess you're my kind of weirdo."

That wasn't enough for him. He pulled out his wallet and opened it to his driver's license, pointing to the photo. "This is me. Take a photo if you'd like."

She glanced at the ID. "That's you. But I…left my phone next door. I'm actually unplugging this vacation."

Unplugging. What a concept.

"I need your cell number anyway. What if I need you in the middle of the night because I'm in over my head here?"

"Just walk over and knock on my door. But… loudly. *I'm* a heavy sleeper."

"Lucky you." He walked her to the door. "Can we agree not to tell anyone else about the baby?"

"I think that's best. I'll check on you two in the morning."

But between old memories, a helpless baby and a beautiful woman next door, Dean would be lucky to get a wink tonight.

Nothing can overcome love.

He certainly wasn't like the men Maribel met on dating apps.

Maribel mulled those words over as she brushed her teeth and got ready for bed, changing into her 49ers long T-shirt. If she hadn't known any better, she'd have thought those words had come out of her own mother's mouth. Her mother often made such sweeping and general statements, seemingly drawing the world into patches of black and white. No gray.

But Maribel certainly did not expect this Greek Adonis–type man with the chiseled jawline and broad shoulders to utter such words. Or to behave with such tenderness and concern toward a baby. Her heart had squeezed tight watching this big man holding a tiny infant close against his chest, as if he'd single-handedly protect her from the world. He might think he could, but Maribel had news for him. It wasn't going to be easy and almost inevitably result in a pain not easily overcome.

He'd been surly with her since the moment they met, his physical countenance often matching his sharp and pointy words. Narrowed eyes, tight jaw. Rigid shoulders. Until that one sentence, laid out for her like a truth bomb. When he'd said the words, his eyes were soft and warm, his voice rich and smooth as mocha.

Is family reunification a myth?

With those words, he'd poured a metaphorical bucket of ice water over her.

Because she used to believe in families. She once believed parents could be reunited with their children simply because of the deep bonds of unconditional love. Parents were hardwired by biology to love their babies and protect them. She'd believed with all her heart before she came front and center with the gray area: addiction. Mental Illness. Poverty. Now, she still lived in those murky shadows. She wished she could see things differently and, as she had in the be-ginning, with a hope and belief that she could change the world. She now realized she could not.

And if the mother hadn't returned by tomorrow night, Maribel would call the police. Dean wouldn't take it well, and there was no point in preemptively starting an argument by revealing her plan. For now, she'd agreed to do this his way. It certainly didn't mean he would *always* get his way. By tomorrow night, maybe this wouldn't be an issue. The mother would be back, or the baby would be on her way to a competent foster home with a loving couple prepared to keep and nurture a baby.

She settled on her bed, pulling out her book to read before she went to sleep. Recently, on the ad-vice of a friend who wrote a book and ran a website on avoiding burnout and rediscovering your pur-pose, Maribel had returned to print. Normally she read everything from her phone app, but accord-ing to her friend, she'd inadvertently zapped herself out of the joy of reading. Her goal here was to slow down, take her time, touch the paper pages and flip through them. Reading was an experience for more than one sense. It could be both tactile and visual. She'd somehow lost the joy of taking her time with something she loved.

Last week she'd visited Once Upon a Book with Stacy and loaded up on novels with happy endings. If it had a dog on the cover and a couple lovingly smiling, it got purchased. Some of her friends loved the raunchy and realistic stuff about the agonizing pain of breakups. If a book made them ugly cry, it became a forever favorite. Not Maribel. She'd had enough of real life. When she'd wanted to cry, when she wanted a knot in her stomach that wouldn't go away, all she'd had to do was read her case files.

In the first few days of reading print books again, she became aware of two things: her focus was lacking, and she almost didn't have the patience to slow down enough to *read*. So she continued to work at it one page at a time. This week on the beach under an umbrella. In fact, she'd had a quiet week until the baby showed up.

Outside, the sounds of soothing waves rolled in and out, and Maribel focused on turning the pages of her book. In no time at all, she was in the mountains of Humboldt County, where a handsome farmer had taken in a divorced mother of two looking for a new start. Sleep came easily, enveloping her in warmth.

The next morning, Maribel blinked, stretched and listened through the thin wall connecting both cottages. No baby crying. Hardly any noise at all outside. Only a sense of disturbing awareness pulsing and buzzing through her body that she couldn't ignore. Maribel could almost hear her sister Jordan's voice in her head.

Time to admit a few things.

Okay, yes, I'm attracted to the grumpy man. So what? Who wouldn't be?

He exuded alpha male confidence, and it had always been her lot in life to fall for the difficult men. For the ones with permanent scowls and surly attitudes. She couldn't seem to fall in love with someone sweet and kind like Clark, her nicest ex-boyfriend, who'd told her in no uncertain terms, "I'm sorry, Maribel, but you are sucking the life right out of me."

Ouch.

Maribel wasn't great at dating, having spent most of her childhood studying. It wasn't that she was trying to prove something, but early on, Maribel realized her strengths were in textbooks. Whether it was science, math or history, she slayed it. Testing wasn't an issue for her. Blessed with a nearly photographic memory, academia wasn't difficult. Boyfriends, at the time, were. This meant that essentially, she was a little socially hindered when it came to romantic relationships.

She'd tried online dating, setting up her profile on Tinder and the others. One of the men had turned out to be married, making her paranoid enough to check for wedding ring tan lines from that point on. One man had arrived at their coffee date looking perfectly presentable. Slacks, dark button-down, loafers. A face with good character, if not particularly handsome. No tan line. After ordering, he called himself a naughty boy, said he had to be punished from time to time and wanted a dominant woman.

She left without finishing her coffee, went home and removed her profile from that particular dating app.

Now, she went to the kitchen to make coffee, the quiet of the morning reverberating all around her. Dressing quickly, she walked next door to check on the baby. Dean had left the door unlocked, so she let herself inside. Tiptoeing through the connected rooms to the bedroom, she found the baby sound asleep in the drawer wrapped in blankets, her little fisted hands bracing her face, her sweet mouth softly suckling in her sleep.

Dean lay on his back on top of the blankets, wearing board shorts and—*oh my*—no shirt. He'd thrown one arm over his face like he wanted to block everything out. Suddenly, he sprang up on his elbows, eyes squinting into the brightness.

"What? *What?*"

Maribel startled and took two steps back. She hadn't said a word and, in fact, was barely breathing. He wasn't kidding about being a light sleeper.

"It's just…me," Maribel squeaked and held up both palms, surrender style. "Sorry. I woke up early and wanted to check on you two. Go back to sleep."

He ignored her and instead walked around the bed to check on the baby.

"She's doing fine," Maribel whispered. "You can relax."

"Now she's sleeping better than I did." He ran a hand down his face. It was only then she realized he'd gathered his hair into a short ponytail.

He had a good face, chiseled jaw and irresistible stubble.

Down, girl.

"Rough night?" She swallowed.

"She was up at two in the morning wanting… something. Gave her a bottle, but she just wanted to be… I don't know…held?" He scratched his chin, and the stubble made a low sound.

"So, you didn't get much sleep?"

"No big deal. Haven't slept well in a while. You?"

"Like a baby. A very nice rest, thanks."

It wasn't entirely true. She'd lain awake for an hour thinking about the baby. About Dean. The mother and whether or not she would return. Whether or not Maribel was doing the right thing giving her a chance to return before involving the authorities.

"Got news for you. Apparently, babies don't sleep. Kind of like me. If you slept well, you did *not* sleep like a baby."

"That could be why you're grumpy all the time." She cleared her throat when he gave her the side-eye. "What do you do about it?"

"I don't take medication if that's what you're asking."

"No, there's melatonin, which is natural. Personally, I recommend reading before bedtime. Something light and happy."

He turned to study her then, his amber eyes appearing darker near the irises. Well, if he was going to stare, she would stare right back. She wasn't intimidated by good-looking dudes with hot bodies. If someone looked away first, it wouldn't be *her.*

Let that be him. She met his eyes. With a baby between them and the fact it was morning, she couldn't escape the unnatural intimacy of the moment. She was in his bedroom just as he'd rolled out of bed. He stood at her elbow, arms crossed, so close her bare elbow brushed against his naked and warm skin.

And it seemed that a live wire lay sparking between them.

One half of his mouth tipped up in a smile. "How did I do? Did I pass the health inspection?"

Still meeting his gaze, she cleared her throat. "You did fine, obviously."

The gaze he slid her made bells and whistles go off in her head. Her body buzzed, and her legs tightened in response to the hint of a smile on his lips. Smiling, she'd decided, was overrated. Better than a smile was the start of one. The way it began in the eyes, moving slowly. Like a teaser of "coming attractions."

Damn it!

She looked away first, too unnerved by the blatant invitation in his eyes.

"Okay! I see everything is good in here. I'll make her a bottle for when she wakes up, and I can take her next door."

She thought she heard him mutter, "Chicken," as she quietly walked away.

Chapter Four

Maribel prepped a bottle for Brianna, then stood to warm it when she heard sounds coming from the back room. Dean emerged a few minutes later dressed in jeans and a T-shirt, swaying a bit as he walked. He held the baby to his shoulder, patting her back, looking a bit like a man in love. She'd moved him up to number one most difficult man she'd ever met, but this morning he slipped back down to the top five.

Maribel handed him the bottle. "So, um, I take it you've already changed her?"

"Yep. We've been getting acquainted. She took pity on me, and this time I only needed one diaper."

"That was kind of her. I'm sorry I wasn't much help last night, but it looks like you've got it handled."

Maribel would feel guilty, except his stepping up

simply reinforced her belief. Dean could be trusted. *See? I've still got good instincts about people.* This was good. It was building back her trust in humanity. He studied her from under hooded eyes. Sleepy eyes. Unfortunately, the whole bedroom eyes look only made him more attractive.

"You'll have to tell me your secret," he said.

"My secret?"

"I have major sleep envy."

"Oh. Well, the book I'm reading puts me to sleep."

Last night, she'd been transported to a small town in the Pacific Northwest. The heroine was learning how to manage and work the strawberry farm her grandfather left her in his will. Maribel had vicariously lived the heroine's fascinating life. She wanted to sink her hands into the loamy earth and pick berries from the bushes. She, too, wanted to fall in love with a handsome farmer.

Dean quirked a brow. "It's boring enough to put you to sleep?"

"Not at all. That *soothing*. It takes me to my happy place, and I can easily drift off to sleep with those pure and lovely images in my head."

"Not sure it would work for me," he grumbled.

"Not with that attitude. And you never know until you try." She rose, going toward him to take Brianna "I'll take her next door. You deserve a break."

"You don't have to watch her all day. We only got her last night. Let's make the babysitting schedule fair and square."

Though this should be her duty and hers alone, she couldn't turn down the help when so freely offered. And frankly, taking care of a baby all by herself scared her a little bit. A lot more than it had spooked Dean, apparently.

"I might take you up on that."

After all, she'd neglected to take a shower before she'd foolishly raced over. It might be tough to take a shower with a baby in the house. Hopefully she'd sleep long enough, but now she'd have to wait for Brianna's nap time. Poor planning. Maribel stepped outside into the cool salt-scented morning air, and Dean braced his arms in the opened door frame.

At that very moment, Maribel noticed her sister-in-law, Ava Del Toro, standing outside her cottage next to Dean's, her hand poised to knock.

Ava's gaze flitted wildly between Dean and Maribel. "I thought… Isn't this your…um…"

Maribel exchanged a quick glance with Dean, which she hoped silently imparted that he should simply back away and not say a word.

He winked and closed the door.

"No, you're right." Maribel skipped over to her cottage and opened the door. "This unit *is* mine."

Ava held a cup of coffee in each hand, her jaw gaping. "You…you have a baby."

"Yes, I do." Inside, Maribel settled on the couch with Brianna. "Ava, listen, it's not what you think…"

"I don't know what I think. When did *you* get a baby?" Ava handed her a coffee.

"It's not my baby, of course. I'm just babysitting. Helping someone."

"Oh, the dude next door?" Ava hooked her thumb.

"Yes." Well, Maribel wasn't lying. Not entirely. "Exactly."

"Well, look. None of *my* business! Max has trained me well. He always says, 'Baby, is that any of your business? Who cares if Sabrina is going out with Roy, but last week, she was dating David?' And I admit he's right. I just know almost everyone in town, and boy, people talk too much! Especially to me." She laughed and held up a palm. "Oh, and don't worry, I won't tell Max."

"There's nothing to *tell*. I just met the man. His name is Dean Hunter, and he's visiting from out of town."

"He's very handsome in that blond surfer kind of way. Not my taste, but I can see the attraction. I *thought* he looked familiar. He's the guy who's been at the bar almost every night. Cole says he's been coming in for a while, usually during the summer."

"Right. That's probably him. Anyway, I'm sure you're wondering…if nothing happened between us, and there's nothing to say…why did I walk out of my next-door neighbor's cottage this early in the morning? And that's a good question!"

Ava smiled and shook her head. "I don't need to know."

"It's complicated. He needed some help. Some, uh…assistance. And advice. Encouragement. You know, typical guy, kind of clueless when it comes to babies."

Ava cocked her head. "Really? Both Adam and Cole know exactly what they're doing."

"Well, he's a cowboy, so who knows? Maybe it's different on the farm. Anyway, he had some questions because she wouldn't sleep, and so I went right over to help. Poor dude. He needs a break."

Brianna, who was quietly observing them both while chomping on her pacifier almost seemed to give Maribel a censuring look.

"How kind of you. Wow, Maribel, you really go above and beyond the call of duty. Even on vacation."

"*Tell* me about it. Anyway, all's well that ends well. Do you mind if I take a quick shower? Um, Brianna spit up on me."

The last part was said in case Ava thought Maribel was trying to shirk her responsibilities. Brianna was an angel who, far from spitting up on her, had given her a drooly smile.

"Oh, I'd love to hold the precious baby." Ava settled on the couch and opened her arms.

"I'll be right back, and then we can talk some more."

In the shower, Maribel soaped up and rinsed off the guilt, both from not telling Ava the full truth, and also lying to Dean. She'd allowed him to believe she'd wait two weeks for the mother to return when she had every intention of calling law enforcement later today. But there was still the slimmest chance the mother would return, and then it wouldn't be an issue. She clung to that hope.

Because he was going to *hate* her if she called the police. He would call her every ugly name in the book of cowboy curse words. But he didn't know Maribel's little secret: she'd already been called every name in the book by angry parents who had viewed *her* as the reason they were separated from their child. Talk about killing the messenger.

So, yes, while it would hurt for Dean to feel she'd betrayed his trust, it wasn't anything she couldn't handle.

"This is delicious as usual."

Maribel took another sip of the perfectly brewed beans Ava specialized in. Her coffee brews were never bitter, and Maribel optimistically called them low calorie, because she didn't need to add cream or sugar for the coffee to be palatable.

"How are the grand opening plans coming along?"

"The honeymoon and settling into married life slowed us down, but now the entire building is fully renovated. We're right on track to open the Green Bean. Max is tracking a storm headed our way, but it shouldn't affect our plans. Other than the handsome single dad next door, how else is your vacation going?"

Maribel swallowed, the bitter taste having everything to do with the lie and not the beverage.

"Good, good. I'm reading about a book a day."

"See? Why read tragic stories that stay with you for a long time? I did that once for my book club. Never again. For a week, Max wanted to know why I was so depressed. I couldn't bring myself to tell him it was because the characters in my novel loved each other but couldn't ever be together."

"Max would have had a good laugh about that. You should have told him."

"Honesty is one thing, but there's such a thing as oversharing." Ava laughed and bent over the baby, who was kicking her legs happily. "Brianna is so adorable. She doesn't look anything like her father. Where's her mother, do you think?"

"Yeah, I'm not entirely sure." Maribel wouldn't meet Ava's eyes.

"Maybe she's adopted?"

"Mmm-hmm," Maribel said.

Guilt continued to relentlessly spike through her. Maribel had been mulling over something Ava said earlier. Ava happened to know a lot of *people* in town. As the president of their local chamber of commerce, she was forever coming into contact both with business owners and customers. Almost every single resident. She might know the baby's mother. That alone was worth telling her the truth, not to mention that Maribel didn't like lying to Ava.

Maribel took another sip of the rich, dark coffee and closed her eyes to enjoy the moment. In addition to trying to undigitize her life, she was also practicing mindfulness. She would enjoy every moment, relish every smell, sight, taste and sound. Especially when drinking and eating.

When she opened her eyes, Ava was sweetly kissing the baby's cheek.

And the lie broke.

"Okay, so listen. I lied to you earlier because this whole situation has me very uncomfortable. Next door? This is not his baby."

Ava's eyes went wide as Maribel told her the whole story. Baby left on the doorstep. The note. The fact her neighbor wanted to help the mother by keeping the baby, but Maribel believed otherwise. Almost on cue, as though she knew they were discussing her fate, Brianna began to fuss in Ava's arms. Maribel took her from Ava and began to rock and sway her.

"We're on either side of this dilemma, but the baby was left on *my* doorstep."

"Can I see the note?"

Maribel reached for the note they'd left on the breakfast bar yesterday and watched as Ava's face grew even paler. "Why you? Do you know her?"

"I have met a few people between my trip here for your wedding and spending time at the bar. Everyone knows I'm Max's sister. And you're obviously the reason I got the last cottage available for rent."

"Do you remember talking to anyone about your work?"

"I might have, probably the last time I was here."

Mostly, she didn't talk about her former career. The last year and the case that had her questioning her abilities made her wonder every day whether she'd wasted years of her life trying to make a difference.

The wheels in Ava's Princeton-educated mind were turning. She studied the note, her finger tracing the words. "Poor thing."

"Do you have a safe haven in Charming? I know you only have a volunteer fire department, but there must be some place…"

"We *don't*. And I feel terrible about this! I'll rally the troops, and we'll get a safe haven established here so this never happens to a baby again. How awful."

"That sounds amazing, really, but the thing is, I need to find this baby's mother. Soon. If I call the police and report this, the clock begins to tick. Within forty-eight hours, the baby will be placed with foster parents. The mother might never see her child again. In the best outcome, she'll have weeks of paperwork and red tape."

"Oh no. You can't *do* that. Maybe she'll be back, just like she said. After all, why else would she write the note?"

She would have expected nothing less from her empathetic sister-in-law, who looked on the bright side of everything. But Ava had a point, which for reasons Maribel didn't quite understand, she accepted far better than when nearly the same words had come out of Dean's lips. After his derision of the system she'd once been a part of, she'd automatically become defensive.

He'd probably heard one of those horror stories that made its way through popular culture once every decade or more. Stories of abusive foster homes. The facts were that most abuse occurred in the *family* home, not the other way around. But positive news stories on either side didn't make juicy and titillating headlines.

"If I could just talk to her, I might be able to help her."

"Do you think she's in trouble?"

"She could be if she's very young. I have no way of knowing. She pulled a pretty desperate move, and that's what worries me."

"I don't personally know of anyone who's recently had a baby other than Valerie and Cole. But I'll ask around and see what I can find out. There are tourists who come during the off-season. And she knows you, obviously, so that ought to narrow it down."

"Maybe she'll be back today after she realizes what she's done."

"But…you will give her more time, won't you?"

"I don't know." Maribel nudged her chin in the direction of her neighbor's home. "He's in over his head, and maybe I am, too."

"If you work together, you can manage. It's only two weeks. And I'm willing to babysit. Max and I need the experience before we have our own children."

Some troubled parents viewed their children as possessions. Without the ability to be impartial, they kept children with them even when the situation they were in was harmful. But at least this young mother had the courage and empathy to give her baby over to what she believed to be a safe and temporary place.

It wasn't much, but it was something.

"I'll think about it."

Chapter Five

Even if Dean had never actually appreciated silence, after Maribel and Brianna left, he heard it ringing loud and clear, like a silent bomb. It was the waiting kind of quiet.

Too quiet. He hated the damn blasted quiet.

In his childhood home, chaos had always followed the silence. He should be relishing the calm, because last night, he'd been through hell on a passport.

The baby wouldn't stop crying around two in the morning. Dean had no idea what he'd done wrong. He'd changed her diaper, fed and burped her. Handed her the pacifier, which she kept spitting out. Eventually, out of desperation, he'd walked the baby outside to the edge of the shore in the moonlight where she could see and smell the ocean. Where she could feel the cool night air, the breezes calm and light.

When she'd seen the water, Brianna made happy gurgling sounds, and Dean thought the wide-eyed look in her eyes and the way she'd kicked her feet said it all. She couldn't believe anything that large existed. Back inside, he'd entertained her by making goofy faces she seemed to love, given her toothless smiles. And then quite suddenly she began to wail. Loudly. Dean tried everything. He paced the floor, jiggling her the best he could, imitating Maribel's rock and sway. But nothing worked. Holding her in one hand, in the other he searched to learn why a baby might cry for absolutely no good reason.

She cried even louder when he'd put her down, and he was supposed to endure *two weeks* of this. This was a job for three people, let alone one person trying to live their life and take care of a baby, too. It was insane. No wonder her mother needed a break. Maybe if he really put on the charm, he might get Maribel to help him the entire time. Hell, maybe he'd get her to take the baby and let him off the hook.

Finally, by the grace of God, Brianna had worn herself out. All he could do was hold her until her cries subsided. They'd slayed him, those tiny whimpering, hiccupping sounds. This baby missed her mother even if she wasn't fully aware of it. She only understood on a basic microbiological level that her world had changed and shifted. If he didn't help, the world she'd come to know in her young life would never be the same.

His short-term goal was to reunite this baby with her mother. And he needed Maribel on his side to make this happen.

This morning, when she'd walked in the room, he'd felt a pull and attraction he had no business feeling. She'd met his gaze and refused to break it until she may have grown too uncomfortable with the intimacy the moment brought. Poor thing didn't know it was a game he liked to play, and he was an expert. But you didn't rise to the top in rodeo circuits without learning how to stare down your competition and *never* be the first to look away.

She'd looked sweet and soft standing in his bedroom, her wavy dark hair slightly mussed. It sounded like she slept without a care in the world, and damn, how he wanted the same. Even if, conveniently, his strange sleeping hours meant he apparently slept like a baby. Which wasn't good sleep at all. Where had that ridiculous saying come from, anyway? If you slept like a baby, you woke up every two to three hours hungry and pissed at the world.

And every time he remembered that Maribel wanted to call the police, his gut burned, and he grew a little angrier at the world, the frustration refusing to dull. Yes, good. This was what he needed. Anger and hostility toward Maribel. That would cure him of any more sexual fantasies.

He wasn't sure he could trust her not to blab

about this situation. The more people who knew, the greater the likelihood someone would think it their civic duty to involve the law. Yeah, some foster parents were good people who only wanted to help. He understood far better than most. But a child always belonged with his or her biological family if all things were equal.

An hour after he'd showered and changed, Dean walked to the door when he heard the knock, suspecting Maribel already wanted a break. But as he opened the door, a pretty blonde stood next to Maribel. She wore a colorful dress, but not at all like the casual sundresses he'd seen Maribel wearing. This one was less vacation style and more board meeting style. Blood rushed into his veins, his flight-or-fight adrenaline surge kicking in. Had she already called in an official? Maribel might have noticed the death glare in his eyes, because she waved her hand dismissively.

"Dean, meet my sister-in-law, Ava Del Toro."

"Nice to meet you." Suspicion rolled over him like a rogue wave. "I'll take my baby now."

He took Brianna from Maribel and jiggled her. She started to cry. It was difficult not to take it personally. Why did this work before and wouldn't work now?

"She's such a sweetheart," Ava said above the racket. "So *cute*."

"Better when she's not wailing," Dean said. "Maybe she's hungry again?"

Maribel approached him, reaching to gently rub Brianna's back in small circles. "We just fed her."

"Could she already be tired again?" he asked.

"If you've tried everything," Ava said. "She might be overstimulated?"

"That's a thing?" He resisted the urge to search the term.

Overstimulated. As in after a wild ride, the blood still pumping, the energy impossible to tamp down. He'd certainly never cried, but had to do *something* to wind down before he'd tried to sleep. Often that used to mean a beautiful woman in his bed ready and willing to wear him out.

"While Maribel was showering, I may have played a few too many peekaboo games with her. Let me take her and try something," Ava said, taking Brianna from his arms.

She cuddled the baby to her chest, her breasts probably acting like soft pillows. This was an unfair advantage in his opinion. Predictably, Brianna began to quiet almost immediately and within a few minutes had fallen asleep.

"The baby whisperer," Dean muttered.

Ava smiled. "Some things you learn by watching. I've seen both Stacy and Valerie do this."

She handed the baby over to Maribel, then took a seat on the couch and folded her hands in her lap. Though she wore a dress with every color under the sun, something about her screamed official. He saw it in her regal bearing. She sat straight and tall, her pale blond hair shorter and straighter than Maribel's. Cut to just below her neck, in clean angles, not a wisp out of place. She looked every square inch of a government representative.

"I've learned so much by watching my good friends with their little ones," Ava said after a beat of silence. "My husband and I don't have children yet. But soon."

"Well, it's just the two of us. I'm a single dad, and—"

"Save it." Maribel set a dozing Brianna into the basket in which she'd arrived. "She already knows."

His fists clenched. "Damn it, Maribel. We said we weren't going to tell anyone."

"Ava isn't just *anyone*. I trust her completely. Not only is she my brother's wife, but she's the president of the chamber of commerce and is constantly in contact with residents. She could help us find the mother."

Dean harbored no grand illusions that he was ready to be a pseudo father to this baby, or any other child. He wanted to find the mother. If possible, he'd like to find the father, too, and force him to man up.

"She *said* she'd come back."

"I know, but she might also need our help."

"As long as it's actual *help*."

"What's that supposed to mean?" Maribel frowned.

"It means it's not going to help if we remove the baby from her mother's home."

"What *home*, cowboy?" Maribel said. "She might need a home herself."

He didn't allow his thoughts to go there. She'd gone to find someone who could help, he was almost sure of it. "Right. So, the baby goes into foster care and the mother is on her own?"

"I'm trying to help here!" Maribel threw up her palms.

"As long as we help *everyone* involved."

A beat of silence followed their arguing, and Ava stood next to the basket and admired the baby. "I can't promise anything, but I'll try my best. Gosh, she's so beautiful."

Now that she was asleep, of course, she resembled a cherubic angel.

"Thanks," Dean said, then wondered why he had accepted the compliment for her when he had nothing to do with her looks.

Neither woman seemed to think anything of it and gave him a pass on the idiotic statement.

But a moment later, Maribel gave him a significant look. "If we're going to keep the baby until the mother gets back, we might need more help than we realized. Neither one of us knows what we're doing."

"The difference is I'm willing to try." The words were said with a clipped edge he hoped she could not miss.

She did not. "Do you really want to spend your entire vacation caring for an infant?"

She had a point. Last night and this morning had

been a trial by fire, and if he didn't get some sleep soon, he was never going to improve his attitude. He was here to relax. Teach himself how to surf. Add this property to his investments if it resisted the coming storm.

"It sounds like you two need to have a talk about exactly what you're taking on," Ava said. "You'll be making a sacrifice, but what you're doing for a family is so important."

Dean revised his attitude about Ava. Someone in this room understood him.

"That's good advice," Maribel said. "We need to consider how much time this will involve. Twelve hours a day, and that's only if she sleeps all night. Even though I am on vacation, I still have plans. People I want to see while I'm here."

Dean crossed his arms. "I'm willing to do this by myself if that's what it takes."

"And I've told you that she left the baby to me, so I can't let you *do* that."

"If we work together, we can do this. Make a schedule. I'll cover when you're busy, and you do the same for me," Dean said.

"We still don't know if she'll be back later today to get the baby," Maribel said.

"Right." Ava nodded. "It could happen. And in the meantime, I'm going to see if I can find out who the mother might be. If she's a resident, I'll find her."

"We suspect she's young," Dean said. "This was a

spur-of-the-moment decision, probably because she hoped *Maribel* would help her."

He let those words sink in, in case Maribel got any second thoughts. She was elbow deep in this. They both were.

"I suggest you make a list," Ava said. "All the things to consider. From what I understand about babies this age, nights are the toughest. Valerie and Cole take turns getting up with Wade, and I think Stacy and Adam did the same for Tennessee."

Dean and Maribel glanced at each other and spoke simultaneously.

"We take turns."

"One night in my cottage, one night in his," Maribel said.

"Hmm. That makes nighttime rough for at least one of you, but as long as you split it equally," Ava said.

"He's only right next door."

Dean nodded. "Exactly."

"What if the baby gets sick?" Ava said.

This stumped him, and it also seemed to, for once, cause Maribel to have nothing to say in response.

"I'll figure out what to do when the time comes," Dean said. "If it comes."

"Why you? The baby was left on *my* doorstep."

Dean palmed his face. She wanted to argue about everything. "*You* want to take care of a sick baby?"

"I'd probably be better at this than you!"

"Why? Because you have a uterus?"

"There are other things, too," Ava said, breaking them out of their sparring match. "You need baby equipment."

"Maybe we don't. She could still come back tonight," Maribel said, continuing to beat a hollow drum.

"We need baby clothes," Dean said, snapping his fingers. "You forgot to add that to the list when I went to the store."

"So, it's my fault?" She sent him a glare, then turned to Ava. "We'll need a car seat in case we need to take her anywhere."

"Where would we take her? Why can't we just stay here?"

Maribel turned on him, fists clenched to her sides. "Do you have to argue with me about *everything*? We need a car seat. What if something should happen, and we have to rush her to the hospital?"

"I'll take up a collection." Ava held up a finger and moved toward the door, probably anxious to get away from them. "So many people give away the stuff their kids outgrow. I know a few families whose kids are much older. They must have something you can use. Even Stacy and Adam might have a few things."

Dean recognized those names. The pacifier obsessed father from last night.

"But we can't bring Valerie into this. She could feel conflicted as a mandated reporter," Maribel said, and then slid Dean a significant look. "In the state of Texas."

The news sent alarm bells through Dean. "And who the hell is Valerie?"

"Take it easy. She's someone else I trust."

"You seem to trust too many people," Dean growled.

"She's married to my husband's best friend," Ava said. "Cole."

Cole Kinsella was really the only person he'd seen every summer. His father had originally owned the bar before Cole and his friends took it over. They'd renovated and turned it into less of a dive and more of a family place.

"And who is your husband?" Dean pointed to Ava.

"Maribel's brother, Max Del Toro."

"One of the bartenders." Dean nodded.

Both Maribel and Ava chuckled.

"He does that, sometimes, though it's best if Cole or one of the others fills in," Ava said.

"Yeah, I got the feeling," Dean said.

And it made sense now. It ran in the family. Brother and sister had plenty in common that went beyond their looks. They were both easily irritated, short-tempered and argumentative.

"I'm going to go," Ava said. "But please call me to babysit if the mother doesn't come back tonight. I would love to cuddle more with this little one."

Dean walked Ava to the door, said goodbye, then shut it and turned to Maribel.

"Next time you decide to change our plans, give

me the four-one-one first, would you?" He may have growled.

"No. You're going to have to trust my decisions."

"So, only you know what's best, right? That's why you were ready to call the police yesterday."

He stalked toward the kitchen to start breakfast. If he didn't eat something soon, his attitude would go from grumpy to worse. When he got close to worse, he made himself scarce. But it would be difficult to do in this situation.

"I'm willing to bend and change course when appropriate and warranted. Maybe you should do the same."

He resented the way she had an answer for everything. Little Miss Know-It-All. She wasn't as attractive anymore. Well, sure, she was still beautiful, but maybe he hated her personality. Or something. He wasn't used to women being this disagreeable with him, because *he* was always the difficult one. This was one title he'd rather not compete for.

"I'm going to make breakfast."

Dean chopped potatoes and added spices. In the other pan, he started the eggs.

"Since she's sleeping, I'll wait to take her next door with me. Is there anything I can do to help you?"

"Just relax. I'm almost done here." He turned the potatoes over, making sure they were getting crispy.

"To be honest, some of my brothers already have children, so I've been around babies quite a lot. Still, it's tougher than I'd realized." She took a seat on the table near the kitchenette. "How do you know so much about children?"

"There is one advantage to lack of sleep. Plenty of time to read." He flipped the eggs. "I'd take pills, but I never want to get hooked. Faced enough of that in the rodeo, taking medications for injuries."

"How many injuries?"

Dean decided he'd tell her everything. *Why not?*

"Compound fracture, five years ago." He pointed to his left arm. "Broke my leg twenty years ago, early on before I knew what I was doin'. Kept me out for a year. Let's see…plenty of concussions, but I recovered from all of them. No permanent damage, so you can stop giving me that look. You might have noticed the scar over my eyebrow. Also, an old injury. My knee is not what it used to be. Took quite a beating."

She quirked a brow. "So, basically, you've made a living from being kicked and abused."

"Is that judgment I hear? I made quite a bit of money over the years, more than most high school dropouts will ever see."

Even if he hadn't glanced up, he would have sensed the tension heavy in the air. He didn't want to reveal just how much money he'd made, and he'd bet Maribel thought it would be very little in the long run. For most rodeo cowboys, it was. But he'd been smarter than many and less inclined to ever be poor again.

He'd guess Maribel had her degree. Maybe two.

Certainly, a master's, possibly even a PhD. Most women who were as smart and accomplished as Maribel never had time for him unless they were slumming. It didn't matter. He'd had a rough start but made something of himself. A life and a career that provided for him far better than any other he'd be qualified to do. He refused to let others judge him.

"Does it surprise you I'm a dropout?"

"Yes, I admit it does. You're clearly very bright. Why not further your education so you'd have something to fall back on?"

"I missed some years when I— Never mind." He set a plate in front of her. "Tell me about yourself, Maribel. Other than you're a former social worker with a restaurateur brother. Is everyone in your family educated and rich?"

"You should have seen my salary. It isn't a motivating factor, believe me. I'm still paying off my student loans and will be for several years."

"Is that why you quit? Not enough money?"

She shook her head. "No. I couldn't do it anymore. I tried to help, but in the end… I didn't make a difference. It's time to do something else."

"Interesting. We both ended our careers. My break is permanent."

"What did you used to do?"

"Rodeo."

"You're an *actual* cowboy?"

"That's right. It's a lot more than wearing a hat, I'll have you know."

"So…you quit the rodeo?"

"Nah." He partly slid and mostly slammed a plate on the breakfast bar. "It never happens that way. The rodeo quit me."

Chapter Six

The rodeo quit me.

Maribel wanted to ask, but Dean's face spoke for him: *don't bother.*

She understood difficult subjects, like the one that made him incredibly suspicious of people like her who only wanted to help. People who'd been trained and had experience. She'd give him a little more time to talk about that, but sooner or later, she would have to know. Because, truthfully, on some level, maybe she hadn't entered into this situation simply to prove to herself there had been a need for what she'd formally expected to dedicate her life's career to. She couldn't accept it had been wasted time.

Maybe she had to prove this to him, too.

She had one good thing to say about Cowboy:

he could certainly cook. The concentration on his stony face as he stirred potatoes and eggs was like watching the temperamental Gordon Ramsay at work, the Western version. Dean's cooking abilities were reason enough to have him stick around. Good looks were the second and third reasons. His ability to single-handedly enhance the scenery wasn't the worst thing to ever happen to her. Maribel had always enjoyed beauty. Mountain streams and sunsets were at the top of a long list. Dean was a little like enjoying a glorious sunset. Distant. Untouchable and golden. Add to that a permanent scowl, and you had Dean in a nutshell.

The potatoes—which he chopped with such determination you'd think it was his job—were crispy perfection, the eggs fluffy enough for him to have added cream, though he hadn't. He had sleep envy? She had cooking envy. Maribel had never been known for her skill in the kitchen and had burned the arroz con pollo. Then again, a few other things happened that night that took her attention away. A cowboy and a baby. This could be the title of one of the books she loved to read. In the book, she'd know the story would have a happy ending, but in this case, as in life, she had no clue but had come to expect the worst.

After breakfast, which she thanked him for, Maribel cleaned up the kitchen for his troubles. He'd made a colossal mess, leaving out potato peels, eggshells and butter. Then she picked up Brianna's basket, some diapers, her bottle and the can of formula that had come with her.

"I'll be at the beach if you need me," Dean said.

"It's fine. I won't need you. I think I can handle her."

But, as it turned out, Maribel could *not*.

When Brianna woke at Maribel's cottage, the baby chose to try out the fully developed lungs she'd been gifted with. Maribel gave her a bottle, changed her, rocked her and nearly burst into tears herself when the baby wouldn't stop fussing. Eventually, after lunch, she fell asleep again, and every muscle in Maribel unclenched. Holding her as though she was a bomb that might go off if she got the slightest bit jostled, Maribel slowly lay Brianna down on the bed. She then propped pillows around them both and settled in beside her with a book.

The R in reading stood for relaxation as she fell into a beautifully woven world where conflicts happened, but those obstacles were handled by adults who were not addicted to drugs or alcohol. They were dealt with by fully functioning grown-ups who were in healthy relationships or working toward that outcome without hurting anyone else in the process. At least, never intentionally, but you couldn't help who you fell in love with.

The image touched Maribel because she'd never truly been loved by anyone outside of her immediate family. Not in the unconditional "I love you even when you're stupid" way everyone deserved. She wanted to love a man and have him love her, dysfunction and all. But for the past few years, she'd settled into a routine. It was dangerous to reveal anything but her sunny side, so she tried to conceal it. She wore a mask on most dates until after the third one. If she ever got that far, the mask came off, and coincidentally or not, the man made himself scarce.

She wondered if Dean was here on a break from his real life, too. Whether he was running from a wife or girlfriend. His license had told her he was thirty-six, five years older than her. He might have been in love dozens of times.

Or maybe only once.

Lowering the book, she noted Brianna was still sleeping, which filled her with anxiety. The baby would probably be up all night if she didn't wake her up now. All babies, she seemed to recall, needed a schedule. She wanted to search this online, like Dean had, but that would violate her wireless month. Besides, as her mami would say, "Madre de Dios, last week the internet told me I had a brain tumor!"

Nope. Sometimes it was best not to have access to knowledge of everything under the sun. Maribel would slowly try to impart this wisdom to Dean during their time stuck together. He seemed unnaturally attached to his phone and the desire to figure everything out at a moment's notice by virtue of the world's largest encyclopedia. Whatever she would need to know about babies, she could find out through the process. Just like in the dark ages before the internet. Maribel was trying this new positive thinking thing on for size.

Picking up the landline phone, she dialed her best friend, because rarely did anything of significance happen without Maribel reporting the news to her.

"Hey there." Her sister, Jordan, answered. "Are you enjoying your vacation?"

"Meh." Maribel explained everything from the baby on the doorstep to Dean, her irritating-as-hell neighbor.

"Uh-oh. And he's grumpy and surly? Watch out."

Maribel snorted. "I can handle him."

"That's not what I meant. Grumpy and surly is your *type*. You always fall for those guys. And believe me, eventually your mutual firecracker personalities will burn each other out. It doesn't work. I've told you, find a good guy who will appreciate you. Like Rafe."

Oh, yes. Rafe Reyes was perfection personified in Jordan's book. But not everyone could wind up with their first love.

"First, I'm not looking for a relationship. And second, these so-called good guys say I suck the marrow right out of their bones. I'm sick of wearing a mask to suit them. Take me or leave me as I am."

"That was *one* guy." Jordan paused for a beat. "You're doing the right thing, you know? I know how hard this must be for you, but everyone deserves a second chance."

"The thing is, I remember feeling that way once.

But the hope has been pummeled right out of me. It took years for it to happen, but…here I am."

"Well, what are you doing to fix this?"

Maribel picked up her book. "Fictionally, I'm already there."

"You'll do it, I know you will. Meanwhile, stay away from the grumpy dude. That can't be good for your positive vibes."

Brianna opened her eyes, turned her head and found Maribel. She gave her a toothless smile, batted her fists in the air, and Maribel's heart filled with warmth and love.

"The baby is awake."

Maribel hung up and smiled at Brianna, who kicked her legs and made those little circles in the air with her fists. Maribel had already come to recognize this as Brianna's contented mood.

And she was content most of the time. A good baby, as her mother had said.

"How could anyone ever leave you?" Maribel whispered. "If you were mine, I wouldn't even leave you for a day."

Later, as the sun began to set, Maribel optimistically gathered everything Brianna had come with and set it by the door in preparation. The mother would be back, and all the things she left would go back with her. Maribel would throw in more diapers and all the formula. She'd certainly have a talk with the mother about support systems. She'd give her a business card and offer to connect her with resources in Texas. Everything would be okay when Maribel saw the regret in the mother's eyes. No harm done. Forgiveness would be given. She'd come back for her baby, and that was all that mattered.

After a few minutes, Maribel stood with Brianna by the window to wait. She looked for any sign of someone lurking in the softly lit shadows of twilight, too shy and humiliated to face Maribel and admit what she'd done.

She opened the front door and walked to the edge of the property, looking in both directions.

Scanning the horizon for…someone.

"Where's Mommy?" Maribel whispered.

Brianna cooed and seemed to be looking, too. No sign of anyone other than the sailboats in the distance and the sounds of the seagulls nearby. And after a few minutes, it was time to admit the truth.

She didn't show.

Maribel heard a door shut and noticed Dean had come outside. He crossed the shared path. "Something wrong?"

"Sh-she's not coming back tonight. I don't think she's coming back."

"I know."

"I'm getting so *tired* of hoping."

"Don't give up on her yet."

"How could she stay away from her baby?" She gazed down at Brianna, her innocent wide eyes flitting between Dean and Maribel as if she, too, wanted to know the answer. "She's so precious."

"It's hard to say." Dean shook his head. "Just… have a little faith."

A single tear slid down Maribel's cheek, followed by another. Then another.

She wiped one away with her free hand. "I'm trying."

"I know that, too." Dean wrapped his arm around Maribel's shoulder, giving her a sideways hug.

It was a welcome surprise. Kind of nice, the warmth of his embrace. His big, firm hands lowered to her waist where they lingered. She ignored the buzzing sensation rippling through her body.

The last of the sunlight disappeared down the horizon as all three of them stood at the edge of the lane.

Waiting.

Two days went by. Maribel spent the next day either reading on the beach under her big umbrella or attending the yoga class in town held at Once Upon a Book. They were struggling to keep their doors open and hosted all manner of events to drum up business. Stacy Cruz, the local *New York Times* bestselling author in town, often held book signings that drew large crowds. But because she wrote one book a year, that wasn't enough to help the local bookstore. The senior citizen Almost Dead Poets Society group hosted poetry readings and single-handedly did their best to keep the doors open.

Today, their teacher was a yogi master named

Dana, who was tall and slim. In Maribel's humble opinion, she had less weight to hold up, so this had to be easier. Meanwhile, Maribel still carried her stress-eating-induced extra seven pounds.

Ava stretched on her mat next to Maribel, following the teacher's instructions.

"How's the baby?" she turned to whisper.

This was Maribel's no-stress space, and she'd been trying not to think about the Brianna issue. It was enough that she thought of her every night and morning and approximately eight hours a day. She'd like thirty minutes to forget.

"His turn today."

Maribel stretched and molded herself into a pretzel and tried to breathe easily and effortlessly.

"No luck finding anyone, sorry," Ava said.

"She'll be back," Maribel said, repeating her daily mantra.

"I'm sure she will. It's been, what, two days?" Ava stretched into downward-facing dog.

Two days, otherwise known as forty-eight hours. This was the length of time afforded as the grace period in which a child could be returned to the mother without being placed into foster care.

A few more stretches, breathing and bending, and the class concluded.

"Namaste." Dana clasped her hands and bent her head.

"Namaste," Maribel said, doing the same.

This was her favorite time. The end. Now, she

could say she'd exercised today. Maribel rolled up her mat and walked with Ava.

They were interrupted by Lois, one of the seniors from the poetry group.

"Girls, your opinions, please. What do y'all think about a yoga poetry class? We would all recite our poems while doing yoga and charge a fee to give to the bookstore."

"Um…" Yoga was hard enough for Maribel without having to recite stanzas at the same time. "Well…"

"That's a great idea!" Ava clapped her hands. "We could make it a yearly event."

Maribel didn't think Ava had ever *heard* of an idea that she didn't like. She walked behind Lois and Ava, happily chatting about poetry and yoga as if the combo was as natural as peanut butter and jelly.

Outside the bookstore, Maribel nearly bumped into a teenager hurriedly walking past her. The same girl she'd recalled seeing in the bookstore once before. Suspicion mounting, she followed her. The teenager glanced back a couple of times, and Maribel thought she caught fear in her eyes. Fear she'd been caught? She followed the girl for a block, then watched as she met another girl in front of the ice cream shop.

Maribel had been following at such a clip that she nearly bumped into them both. Her mat fell to the sidewalk and unrolled between them.

"Damn it!"

"Are you *following* me?" the teenager asked, hurriedly picking up the mat and handing it back to Maribel.

"Don't be ridiculous," Maribel said, her cheeks burning. "I was coming to the ice cream shop. Um, this is my treat after yoga class. I've earned it."

"Ohhh. Riiight." The girl smiled, accepting the pathetic excuse. "Sorry. It just looked like you were following me."

"You watch too much *Dateline*, Ellie," the other girl said.

Ellie and her friend both walked inside, and Maribel was forced to follow.

When she returned to the cottage, she carried with her a quart of cherry vanilla she planned to foist on Dean. Next door in his freezer, maybe it wouldn't tempt her, because right now she wanted to eat the whole thing in one sitting. Just slam it down.

What's wrong with me? She couldn't just assume every teenage girl in town had abandoned her baby. And she couldn't simply believe *only* a teenager would have done such a thing. Her old need to fix things reemerged because it was in her nature. She had to let go of the fixing and start with the living. Right.

She had today, and she would take advantage of it.

Back at her cottage, she shoved the ice cream in the freezer for later and carried her book to the outdoor deck patio. Each unit had an umbrella and table combination with matching chairs. A sandy pathway led to the beach several hundred feet away, separated only by small grassy areas and shrubs.

Two minutes into her book, the heroine was struggling to save the strawberry farm. Years of debts by her gambling addict of a grandfather had destroyed any reserves of money to get through lean times. The heroine was at an impasse. Sell the farm or put everything she had into reviving it? The farmer had his own ideas, too, of going completely green, which meant a lot more money. Frequent arguments with him seemed to be disguising the fact they were both wildly attracted to each other.

"How are you doin', darlin'? Yeah, you know you're beautiful. I know it, too." The smooth drawl came over the outdoor patio adjacent to hers.

Dean. Was he actually entertaining a woman next door or simply on a phone call? Either way, he could at least wait until it was *her* turn with Brianna to start a beach romance.

Maribel whipped around to tell him off when she heard "Just don't spit up on me again, okay?"

Dean was holding Brianna like she was a football and he was poised to make a touchdown in the end zone. Her arms and legs were kicking, and she cooed happily.

"What?" Dean caught Maribel staring at him. "The research says this is good for gas."

"Gas?" Maribel wrinkled her nose.

"Colic. That's a reason babies cry. They have a stomachache."

"Oh." She went back to her book.

Two minutes later, he'd pulled up a chair next to his table only feet away from hers. He sat Brianna on his lap and bounced her.

"What are you reading?"

"I *was* reading my book."

"Yeah, I can see that." He smirked, then turned Brianna to face him. "She doesn't want to show me the book, does she?"

"Stop that."

He quirked a brow.

"Stop talking through the baby. You realize she doesn't understand what you're saying, don't you?"

"Research shows you shouldn't dumb it down with babies. No *baby* talk." He scowled.

"Fine," she grumbled and showed him the cover of her book. "It's a romance."

"Those are the books you were talking about?"

"Yes, exactly. Very soothing and calming. My happy place."

Now, if she could just get back to it, but both baby and cowboy were one monumental distraction. Today, at least, Dean wore a shirt. One that strained against his biceps, however, which wasn't as helpful as she might have hoped.

"Do you have one I could borrow?" he asked.

She stared at him blankly. "Are you serious?"

"Sure, I'm willing to try it. The worst that could happen is it doesn't work for me, and I still can't sleep." Brianna blew a raspberry at Dean. "I said no spitting on me, darlin'."

She cooed and squealed. Dean smiled, and it was filled with such warmth that Maribel's pulse kicked up. He was just…unfairly attractive. At least to her.

Opening the sliders to her cottage, Maribel walked inside and reached for a book from her stack. Just for fun, she chose a Western with a handsome cowboy on the cover.

"Here."

He frowned. "A Western?"

"Yes. A Western romance."

"Did you give me a Western because I'm a cowboy?"

"Maybe. I thought you could relate to that world."

"Sure," he said, not appearing at all certain. He set it on his table.

Maribel went back to her book and the strawberry fields, ignoring them both with a Herculean effort.

Chapter Seven

The next morning, Maribel had just rolled out of bed when she heard a knock on her sliding glass door. She swished back the drapes, and there stood Dean, wearing aviator shades and board shorts with no shirt. Seemed to be his uniform. He held Brianna, a beefy arm across her belly, and faced Maribel.

The baby stuck a fist in her mouth and gave Maribel a *You again?* look.

"Mornin'." He whipped off his shades and quirked a brow, no doubt at her state of dress.

She probably had wild bed hair and still wore her jammies with no bra.

"Barely." Slowly, she undid the locks and slid open the glass doors.

"She had a wicked diaper this morning. Disgusting. I gave her a bath in the sink. You're welcome," Dean said, passing the baby over.

Every now and again, it seemed he was trying to one-up her to take the Babysitter of the Year Award. Or maybe that was just her and her competitive spirit. When you were raised in a family of six, you had to fight to be noticed some days.

Without even realizing what she was doing, Maribel took in a nice whiff of Brianna's sweet baby scent.

"Smells good, right?" Dean winked.

"Um, yeah. I actually didn't expect you this early."

"I see that." He stepped inside. "I know what it's like to be overwhelmed. You obviously need a break."

She bristled at the idea that she couldn't take care of Brianna with the same ease *he* seemed to. But she had found herself competing in a contest she hadn't even wanted to enter.

He took the baby from her. "Go ahead. Take a shower and get dressed. I'll sit with her until you're done."

But taking a shower with him in the same house seemed a bit too intimate. She'd been careful not to barge in on him and the baby again the way she had the first day. The buzzing sensations in her body, the tight awareness of him, were things she hadn't signed up for on this vacation. She had the distinct impression he'd already showered, which meant he'd done all this before Brianna woke up. One more point to Dean.

She cocked her head and studied him. "Are you *sure* you've never had a kid?"

He chuckled. "Funny, but I think I would remember that."

"Do you have a sister or brother who has kids?"

"Nope. No sister. No brother." He sat on her couch, holding Brianna in the crook of his elbow. "Only child."

"Are you married?" The question came out before she could stop herself.

"What?" His neck swiveled back. "Why would you ask me that?"

"Nice way to avoid answering. Answering a question with a question. Don't think I didn't notice."

With what could only be called a double scowl, he held up his left ring finger. "Look closely, genius. No tan line."

Oh, and she did check for the tan line.

"I just wanted to know if I'd be dealing with a jealous wife showing up wondering why we're practically playing house."

"No wife. No girlfriend or significant other. I'm a free and single man. Anything else you want to know?"

Your fascination with surfing? What's it like on the farm? Do you own a horse? Is ranch life just like in the books?

"I was in a relationship, but it's over," he added after a beat.

The honesty surprised her. Most men wouldn't feel the need to add the qualifier.

"Are you sure?"

"Positive. I guess I almost married her." He shrugged.

He'd *guess* he almost married her?

"But there's something about cheating that sours the relationship."

"Your cheating or hers?"

"Hers."

Oh, jeez. Poor Dean, and funny how he didn't even remotely look like the kind of man anyone would cheat on. Humans were a strange bunch, and so much of their decisions didn't follow logic. Another reason she preferred books. Everything in them made sense.

"Oh no. I'm sorry, that's a tough break. I hope you got closure." She was almost sorry the moment she'd said it. The counseling side of her was unrelenting some days.

Let it go. This is how you lose boyfriends and friendships.

"Closure?" He chuckled. "Is that therapy speak?"

"No, not necessarily *therapy*. You don't need therapy unless you want to work things out, but closure can help you to move on. Just the ability to take a look at what led the two of you to that place, why she felt the need to get your attention in such a way."

His brow furrowed as if he were trying to evaluate whether he should take her seriously or not. "No closure. Honestly? I haven't spoken to her since."

"You're kidding, right?"

"Not kidding. I have nothing to say to her." He brought Brianna to his shoulder and patted her back until she burped. "Has it ever happened to you?"

"Has *what* ever happened to me?"

He gave her a look. "Anyone ever cheat on you? Break your heart?"

"To tell the truth, I always seemed to just miss them. You should see how many of the swipes I had on Tinder were from married men who must think I look like a whole lot of fun."

"Yeah?" He started scrolling through his phone. "I'll need to see your photo."

"No, you don't."

"C'mon. The profile photo is everything."

"It's just a professional photo of me, not like I'm naked or anything."

"No, that's not allowed."

"So, *you're* on Tinder."

"Nah, the rodeo circuit has its own version of Tinder."

She quirked a brow. "I've heard the stories. Buckle babes? Is that what you call them?"

"Buckle bunnies. You're cute, you know?"

"Cute. Yes, a cute woman who gets hit on by married men. Once it happened, Max started giving every single one of my dates a criminal background check."

"If I had a sister, I'd do the same. Have *him* check out your photo. I guarantee you, there's something about your profile or photo that must be off. Or maybe something in your bio."

"That's where you're wrong." Finally, she relented. "Give me your phone."

He handed it to her, and she brought up a site, found her profile and handed him his phone. "See? I used the same one as on my LinkedIn profile. Just me wearing one of the pantsuits I wear to work. My hair tied up in a tight bun. Very professional."

He did a double take. "Jesus. It's the sexy librarian look all the livelong day. No *wonder*."

"What are you *talking* about?"

"And you're wearing glasses, too. It couldn't get much worse." Then he started to laugh so hard his shoulders shook.

She took another look at the photo and suddenly saw it through the eyes of a heterosexual male. Normally, she wore contacts but the glasses, she believed, gave her a look of intelligence and authority. Her arms were crossed, a smirk on her face, her head cocked.

Suddenly, the only thing missing seemed to be the whip she'd beat her dates into submission with. The weird guy who'd wanted orders made a lot more sense now.

"Oh my God, I look like a dominatrix. Ugh! Why didn't anyone tell me this?"

But Dean was now wiping away tears of laughter. Brianna, who seemed to sense the mood of her favorite person, kicked her feet and cooed happily.

Maribel shook his phone before tossing it back to him. "You want to know what the problem is with online dating?"

"Pretty sure there's not just one."

"It's pheromones."

He wrinkled his brow. "Pheromones."

"The problem is, there's no way to translate those chemicals through with a simple photo. When I'm able to meet men in real life, it's a different story. Attraction is a chemical thing. It's the dopamine."

"Wow, so you're a romantic."

She made a face. "It doesn't matter anymore. When I get home, I'm shutting down all my profiles."

"Yeah? Good thing. All men are dogs."

"I give up. Maybe I'm not meant to find that 'special someone.'" She held up air quotes.

"Not with that kind of an attitude."

"Are you telling me you *haven't* given up?"

"Not at all. But I'm in no hurry to try again, if that's what you're asking."

This piqued her interest, but his personal life was none of her business. They just had to hang on a bit longer. Until the mother came home.

Or didn't.

Maribel swallowed hard. "Have you even considered the possibility Brianna's mother might not come back at all?"

"I'm not an idiot. We made a deal."

"So, you'll be okay with my calling the authorities and starting the process?"

"I don't see that we'd have much of a choice."

Brianna batted her fists in the air and looked at Dean with eyes that seemed to understand she had someone on her side.

"She likes you."

"Don't you get any ideas. We're still sharing her."

Maribel snorted. "What's wrong? No longer think you can handle her all on your own?"

"You were right and I was wrong. When I took her, I had no idea what I'd gotten myself into. I can already see how tough this is going to be, and of course it wasn't fair of the mother to dump her on you."

Well, at least he was admitting this. And obviously, it wasn't as easy for him as he made it look.

"But you still think we're doing the right thing?"

"Without a doubt. Don't you agree?"

She crossed her arms. "I don't know what to think. It's such an irresponsible thing to do, but I'm trying to understand the mind of the woman who would have done something like this."

"You've probably heard far worse than leaving a baby on the doorstep. There are…awful places."

Maribel didn't want to think of those places where indeed newborns were sometimes found. Far less of these occurrences happened in regions where the Safe Haven law existed. Most of the time, the baby's mother would never be found, and the child went directly into a foster home after the waiting period.

Dean cleared his throat. "You could choose to be flattered. This mother might have carefully considered the safest place for her baby. And it was with you."

The sweet words didn't have a positive effect on Maribel. She wasn't flattered so much as terrified. Being responsible for a baby was much harder than she'd ever imagined. All the foster parents who so kindly gave of their time and dedication were even more amazing to her now.

A knock on her front door disrupted those fleeting and disjointed thoughts, and she heard Ava's voice on the other side: "Maribel! I'm back."

Ava and Max stood outside, both carrying packages.

"Well, that was fast," Maribel said, holding the door open for them to walk inside.

"The people of Charming are some of the most generous you'll ever meet," Ava said with the typical enthusiasm of a born cheerleader.

Max carried in a car seat and set it down. "There's more."

"Let me help." Dean handed the baby to Maribel and followed Max out the door.

Within minutes, they not only had a car seat, but

bottles, more diapers, clothes and what amounted to a portable crib.

"They call it a Pack 'N Play," Ava said. "Part play pen, part crib. No more sleeping in the dresser drawer."

"You were letting the baby sleep in the dresser drawer?" Max sounded incredulous.

"I switched her to the middle of my bed," Dean said with a defensive edge to his tone. "I put pillows all around. She can't fall."

Both men momentarily eyed each other before Max spoke and held out his hand. "Dean, right? You're one of our customers. Saw you at the bar the other night."

Dean shook Max's hand. "That's right. You run a great establishment. I've been coming in since before y'all took it over."

Max nodded. "Cole says you're a surfer."

"I wouldn't go that far." Dean stuck his hands in his pockets, looking almost sheepish. "I try."

"Let me hold that precious baby." Ava took Brianna from Maribel's arms. "Max, come here and look at this baby."

Max obliged, peering down over Ava's shoulder. He cracked a smile, something she'd rarely seen her brother do in pre-Ava days. These days, he often grinned like a loon. Meanwhile, Dean was making himself useful, unpacking the portable crib and carrying it to Maribel's bedroom.

"I'll take some of this stuff over to my place, too,

so it's not crowding you." Dean grabbed a few items and was out the back door with them.

"Don't worry," Max said, suddenly at her elbow. "He checks out."

"Really? Again? I thought we were done with this."

"I have a business, so it's not a problem to run a light criminal check. Also, never been married. He makes the cut."

"There is no cut to *make*. I'm not dating him, I'm not dating anyone ever again, and anyway, you promised you'd stop doing that."

"But you're spending a lot of time together. And the whole baby sharing thing. I *had* to check him out."

"Okay, thanks, but I wish for once you'd trust in my judgment. Do you think I'm crazy? To do…all this?" She waved her hands around the room rapidly filling with baby equipment.

"No. I know you, and I trust your judgment with all this. And, if I ever had any doubts, my wife would of course wipe them all away. You know her and her bleeding heart." Max joked, but there was a sweet tenderness in his voice as his eyes followed Ava as she held the baby and swayed with her.

"It's just temporary. I won't let this become a disaster. This baby is going to get everything she needs."

"I have no doubt now that you're involved."

"Thanks, Max."

Ava joined them, sidling up to Max and carrying a smiling Brianna. "I want one."

"Yeah?" Max grinned and reached to tug a lock of Ava's hair. "I'll see what I can do about that."

Maribel groaned and pulled a face. "Not in front of me you won't."

"Your family is great."

Maribel chuckled. "You almost sound like you mean it."

Dean actually did. After unloading all the donations, the four of them sat and ate a pizza they'd ordered while the baby lay in the carrier someone had donated. It was kind of like a car seat but *not* a car seat. Or at least, he'd been warned within an inch of his life not to use it as such. They'd been given a car seat, too, a stroller and some kind of backpack where you could carry the baby in the front. The amount of paraphernalia involved with having a baby was horrible. He was grateful they could spread it out between two small units.

"You can be honest. My brother is a lot to take. He means well, but he's a bit of an alpha, always the bull in the room."

"Must be why I like him. I'm rather fond of bulls."

"Yeah, I guess you would be. He can also be a grump, just like you."

"Is that where you get it from? Must be hereditary. You give as good as you get."

In talking to Max, Dean learned Maribel was

part of a large Latino family of two sisters and four brothers. They'd been raised in the agricultural community of Watsonville, California, not far from the Pacific Ocean. Max had enlisted in the navy after high school, rising through the ranks to become a SEAL. As for Maribel, she'd always been a good student, acing high school to graduate as the valedictorian. With an academic scholarship to UC Davis, she'd studied psychology and later earned her PhD. As he'd suspected, Maribel was as smart and accomplished as they came. No surprise to him.

After Max and Ava left, Dean and Maribel unpacked the baby clothes and sorted through the donations. Then she hand-washed all the baby bottles donated, filled them with formula and organized them in the refrigerator. She gave him half to take over to his place. This planning ahead thing was genius. Not for the first time, Dean reminded himself he was lucky Maribel hadn't left him to fend for himself.

But the strange type of forced intimacy with someone he'd only just met felt…odd. He'd been on the road for most of his adult life, usually on his own, except for the random companionship of the occasional buckle bunny. The lifestyle of the road went right along with the chaotic way he'd been raised, and it fit. Until it didn't.

Dean glanced at his nautical watch. He'd been tracking a hurricane off the Gulf Coast for the past few days. It was expected to miss them, as most hurricanes had for the past one hundred years. But they would get some rain and high winds. Possibly a loss of power if the surge came any closer, but he highly doubted it.

Making himself useful, he grabbed a ready bottle from Maribel's fridge and stuck it in a warm pan of water. It struck him they were already becoming a well-oiled machine, just like on a ranch. Everyone had a job. He considered most couples with children could learn something from them. Cooperate, assign, split up tasks, get things done. Don't get all caught up in the minutiae.

Of course, all this would be a lot easier if she didn't open the back door wearing nothing but a long T-shirt and bed hair. Maribel had a soft morning look about her that had him engaging in some fairly steamy fantasies. And the book she'd given him to read wasn't helping matters. Those people were having a lot of fun, and he hated only reading about it.

Dean moved to the back door to leave, but before he did, he would test his new theory. A day ago, she would have told him to go jump off a cliff if he offered his help. She would have told him she didn't need his directions and ask him to please stop mansplaining every little thing.

"Don't forget to burp her," he said now. "I think trapped gas makes her cry."

"Oh, right." Maribel brought the baby to her shoulder and patted her back.

Yeah, safe to say she no longer *hated* him. Other

than those two initial meetings in which he found her so full of herself, Maribel had a sweetness about her not many would assume lay under her kickass facade. He saw it in the way she affectionately teased her brother, whom she obviously had a serious case of hero worship for. He saw it with the baby, in the way she held her close to her bosom. And despite her reservations, she'd owned up to the fact the baby was *her* responsibility. He admired the ability to admit to a mistake.

A moment later, she glanced up at Dean. "I got nothing. Isn't she supposed to burp by now? Why isn't she? What am I doing wrong?"

"Take it easy, boss." Dean reached over and patted her back a few times, too. "You're not doing anything wrong."

A moment later, the baby made such a loud and resounding burp that both he and Maribel burst out laughing.

He chuckled. "Even she looks surprised that sound came out of her."

Brianna's eyes were wide and bright as she took them both in.

"The mother was right. She's a good baby."

"She'll be back for her. I know it." He squeezed Maribel's shoulder.

He attempted to reassure Maribel every chance he got that she'd done the right thing, that she was doing the right thing.

And he fervently hoped they both were.

"I hope you're right," Maribel said with such sadness in her eyes that he wondered how she'd become so jaded.

Maybe he didn't want to know.

Chapter Eight

Brianna did *not* sleep peacefully in the portable crib beside Maribel's bed, waking once during the night and fully awake at five the next morning.

"I wish you'd get your days and nights straight," Maribel muttered, suddenly aware she was talking to a baby. "What am I doing? You don't understand, do you?"

"Coo!" Brianna said and kicked her legs.

"Let's go take you back to your favorite person."

Outside, the skies had turned gray, clouds looming over the horizon. Rain was forecasted, and Max had warned her about a tropical storm that might hit the area, assuring her many times that she had nothing to fear. No hurricane, in other words.

Maribel delivered Brianna next door, Dean answering the door again without his shirt. This had become annoying. She briefly wondered how he'd react if *she* opened the door to her cottage not wearing a shirt.

Never mind. He was a heterosexual *guy*. He'd probably enjoy that very much.

"Mornin'," he said, rubbing his eyes with the heels of his hands. "I'm going to need the crib thing since it's my turn to have her tonight."

Dean grabbed a T-shirt and pulled it over his head. He then took Brianna from Maribel, strapped on the baby backpack and slipped Brianna right into it as if he'd been doing it all his life. She watched, dumbfounded for a moment, until she realized what he'd done.

"Wait a second. Did you search online how that contraption works?" It had so many belts and buckles Maribel thought she'd have a hard time figuring it out.

"YouTube," he said without missing a beat. "It's actually much simpler than you would think."

"Well, I guess you understand buckles. And belts."

She turned to get the portable crib, and he followed her next door.

He quirked a brow. "Any updates?"

"No. Just woke up early as usual. And, hey, I know it's my turn to watch her tomorrow, but I'm invited to Ava's grand opening, so would you…?"

"Sure."

"Thanks, buddy." She waved and watched as he carried both the baby and the portable crib next door.

Free for now, the rest of the morning passed with a yoga session courtesy of YouTube's reigning queen, because supposedly, all this bending, stretching and breathing was good for mindfulness. Good for all this unplugging she'd been doing. Good riddance to all forms of electronics and social media! She didn't miss *any* of it. In fact, she was calmer, more at peace, without the dreaded FOMO.

Despite the coming storm, or maybe because of it, she cooked like crazy in the kitchen, making an ambitious attempt at paella. It failed miserably when she burned the rice, but tomorrow was another day.

And then, because she needed a morale boost, Maribel dialed Jordan.

"She didn't show," Maribel said.

Jordan hesitated only a beat. "Did you really think she would?"

"I hoped so! Could either you or Rafe leave Susan with a complete stranger?"

Jordan and Rafe were coparenting with his ex-wife and raising a five-year-old daughter.

"No, of course not. But she's obviously desperate. Remember that not everyone had all the advantages we did growing up."

Maribel wanted to argue this, because all their so-called advantages had come from hard and, at least in her parents' case, backbreaking work. But she'd also had loving and supportive parents who would lay down their lives for any of their six children. Their small and modest home had always been her soft place to fall. She'd been luckier than so many of her classmates, and a pebble formed in her throat at the memory of a particular student. Even if she'd been one of the reasons Maribel went into social work, she hadn't thought of her in years.

After hanging up with Jordan, Maribel grabbed a book and settled down to read. She'd slowed down to reading a book every two days, but it was still wonderful escapism. Pure joy. This new book was set in New York City, with a heroine who worked as a dog walker. Her next-door neighbor was a struggling actor who didn't have enough time for his dog. Perfect. About ten pages into the book, the two were about to meet when the handsome hero was chasing his dog down the busy city street.

And then a knock on Maribel's sliding glass door interrupted the meet-cute. A glance at the clock showed her three hours had passed since she sat down to read. Still no rain outside, only those threatening clouds.

Maribel slid the curtains back and found Dean standing before her in bare feet. He wore board shorts, a T-shirt and a Western hat. It seemed to be a different one every day. How many did this cowboy own?

"A storm is fixing to come soon, and I won't be able to surf. If you're not busy, mind watching her over at my place while I hit the waves?"

"Is that what you call it? *Hitting* the waves?"

"In my case, it's fairly accurate."

"Should you be doing that now? It's going to storm, right?"

"Not yet." He scowled and hooked a thumb to his place. "She's sleeping, so it shouldn't be any trouble for you while I'm gone."

She held up her book to demonstrate she'd been doing something, then jabbed a finger between them.

"Listen, buddy. It's not going to go down this way. You're not going to go off and have your fun while I sit here chained to the baby's every need."

Oh dear, she sounded like a nagging wife.

He cocked his head. "Hey, she's sleeping. Even *you* can handle that."

There he went again, acting as if he could do a better job than she.

"What's that supposed to mean? I'm doing just fine."

"Is that why you looked like you'd been dragged through the mud this morning?"

"I did not look like mud!"

"You looked *tired*. And I get it. Hey, listen. No one can be great at everything."

It was almost as if he knew how those words would affect her. Clearly a feeble attempt at reverse psychology. It was like he'd pushed a whole lot of buttons and finally got to the right one. She hadn't graduated as valedictorian to hear such a blanket statement.

Of *course* she couldn't be good at it all, so she'd excelled in academics. She still had a knee-jerk reaction to being told she couldn't do anything well, but Dean couldn't possibly know this about her. He just seemed to have a talent for stepping on her rawest, most exposed wound.

"So…is that a no, ma'am?" He lowered his chin and studied her from under ridiculously long eyelashes. "Promise I won't be long."

The color flashed in his amber eyes, and it hit her like a gut punch. He seemed to be a magnet she kept getting drawn toward even as she held up her arms and tried to fight it.

But he'd agreed to watch Brianna tomorrow while she went to Ava's grand opening, so it was only fair. Besides, she was reading, and as long as Brianna kept sleeping, it could work. Even if it seemed those old overachieving tendencies of hers were once more rising to the surface.

"Fine."

She sighed deeply and with great flair to show him what a sacrifice she'd make for him by going next door to read. Surfing before a storm had to be better than during one, at least. Either way, she had begun to admire his tenacity.

"Don't be gone all afternoon, or I swear on everything that's holy, I'll hunt you down." She pointed.

He quirked a brow. "I have no doubt."

Taking her book with her, Maribel slipped through the adjoining sliding doors into his cottage and watched Dean stalk down the path to their private beach. Inside, Brianna was snoozing in the portable crib on her side. Dean had rolled a blanket behind her back so she wouldn't roll over on her stomach. Ingenious. This cowboy kept surprising her. He seemed willing to learn and try new things, and maybe she shouldn't be so hard on him even if he had to search online for everything. He never let his lack of information stand in the way of taking action. Maribel tended to study and research a subject to death before doing anything. Including dating guys.

She'd never been great with the opposite sex from the time she'd been the nerdy girl with the thick glasses, nose always stuck in a book. Jordan had been busy falling in love and planning a life with her first love. She was outgoing, pretty and loved a party, while generally speaking, Maribel had loved books and studying. Oh, she'd tried to be more like her sister, but as Jordan continually reminded her: "you have your own strengths and they're valuable."

Maribel settled into a chair in the living room and went back to her story. Once more on the streets of Brooklyn, the hero named Joel and the heroine named Miranda agree that she would watch his dog during the day if he would pretend to be her boyfriend for a huge company party. She flew through a hundred pages and the first amazing electrifying kiss.

Then Brianna woke up with a small cry, and Maribel put the book down, unaware of how much time had passed while she'd been sucked into this other world, but quite frankly, resenting having to leave it. Again.

"Well, hey there." Maribel picked Brianna up from the portable crib. "Your favorite person in the world isn't here, but he'll be back."

She changed the baby's diaper and marveled at how easily she'd fallen into this strange routine of caring for an infant. Once, Maribel's mother had asked her if she'd ever consider becoming a foster parent herself.

"No," she'd answered. "It takes a special person to love and care for a baby and be prepared to give them back."

She'd seen it time and time again. Caring for someone else's baby was the most selfless thing anyone could do.

Suddenly the sliding door slammed open so loudly that Maribel jumped. She glanced up at Dean, who no longer wore his T-shirt, like a shark might have ripped it off him. There seemed to be a cut on his chest. His chin a sharp and angry red, he also had a good start on a black eye.

She settled Brianna in the bouncy seat. "Dear God, what *happened* to you?"

"One of those waves hit me. Hard." He propped the board against the wall, then stalked toward the bathroom.

"And gave you a *black eye*? I didn't know a wave was capable of that."

She followed him, wondering if she would be called on to administer first aid. It wasn't in her nature to stand by and let someone suffer on her watch. But hey, this is what he got for surfing before a storm.

Dean touched his eye with the pads of his fingers and cursed. "This part wasn't the wave. It was the board hitting me as it flew through the air and stopped only when it found my face."

"I'll get you some ice."

"Take care of the baby, I can handle this myself." He slammed the door to the bathroom shut.

How irritatingly *male* of him. The ego on this one! So, he didn't need *her* help. He'd interrupted her quiet time, and now he didn't want her help? Well, he was going to get it anyway! Some vacation she was enjoying. Goodbye quiet time. She'd been called on to rescue a baby and now a cowboy surfer. Next stop, save the world. She marched to his kitchen, rummaged in the freezer and wrapped several ice cubes in a kitchen towel.

The bathroom door was closed, which momentarily stalled her progress. She couldn't just barge in on him because she heard the shower going. He might already be naked. This kind of forced proximity and false intimacy was messing with her head. They were friends, sort of, but he was also very, um, male. *Resoundingly* male.

She knocked on the door sharply.

"What?" he growled from inside.

"I've got ice," she shouted to be heard over the water.

"I'll alert the media."

"If you don't ice that eye, it's going to swell up. Open the door, you stubborn man-child."

"Can't. I'm naked."

Maribel sucked in a breath and had no words. She'd been trying *not* to picture Dean naked with amazing success.

Until this moment.

"I—I have ice," she said, but her voice shook as she pictured those rippling back muscles. Those amazing beefy forearms. She briefly considered dropping the towel to the ground and backing away slowly as if she'd delivered a ransom in a book. "Don't be an idiot. Just open the door a crack and take it from me."

No answer. Then the door swung open. Out of instinct she refused to look, turned her head and thrust the towel toward him. And connected with... something *hard*.

He groaned and cursed. She swiveled to find him rubbing his now pink chin. *Oh, Lord.* She'd hit him with the towel full of ice. That had to hurt.

"I'm s-sorry, but you opened the door!" She flew into a defensive posture, a familiar landscape.

"What's wrong with you? You *asked* me to open the door."

"But you weren't supposed to open the door. You said you were naked."

But he wasn't. Naked, that is. A towel hung low on his hips, threatening to fall off at any moment. In a way, this was worse. Tantalizing to what she couldn't but could almost see. Washboard abs were all she could see, and that was more than enough.

"You're dangerous, woman." He sent her a menacing look as he worked his jaw.

"Ha! Dangerous? Me? Not usually. And you should know I feel *terrible* about this."

"How terrible? Are we talking you'll put me in your will, or are we talking something a little less… permanent?" He slid a look toward the shower, quirked a brow, and an almost-smile tipped one corner of his mouth. "I'm very good in the shower."

Well. How unsurprising. He was at death's door and could still have uncomplicated sex with a virtual stranger. This was the closest she'd seen to what he might look like without a scowl, just the hint of a smile curving his lips, and then and there she determined she better *keep him* scowling. The almost-smile, the spark of mischief in his amber eyes… speaking of dangerous…

"I—I feel only terrible enough to tend to your wounds."

She pushed against him, meeting muscle the consistency of granite. Oh no. That was dangerous. Note to self: don't touch him again.

"Sit *down*."

The shower was steaming up the mirror, and he reached over to shut it off. His back to her, he rummaged through medicine cabinets. Obviously, he was accustomed to injuring himself and had all the proper supplies.

"I told you I'd take care of this." He met her gaze in the mirror. "Don't need your help."

"And I would leave you alone to stew in your manhood, but I did clock you."

"That's some right hook. I'm going to call you Rocky from now on." He turned and relented, handing her the antiseptic and a cotton ball. "Doesn't it bother you that I'm wearing nothing but a towel?"

"I hardly noticed," she lied and applied some antiseptic to the cotton ball. "I'm a professional. I know how to compartmentalize. Necessary for my job. Hold still."

But her hand shook slightly when he closed his eyes, his vulnerability doing strange things to her heartbeat. It raced, then slowed, then raced again. She would need a pacemaker if this kept up.

He opened one eye suspiciously. "What are you doing? It feels like you're brushing a feather over me."

And here was the thing about Dean. While he appeared a demigod from a distance, a golden pretty boy, this close he was a mere mortal. Attractive, yeah, but hardly *perfect*. A scar partially bisected his right eyebrow, where a lock of his hair continually fell in a boyish way. His nose was slightly crooked. He wasn't perfect, but it didn't do a thing to diminish her attraction to him.

"I'm trying to be careful not to further injure you, which I figured you'd appreciate." She dabbed a little harder at his chin, and he winced. "Don't be such a baby. You should have known this would happen."

"How could I *plan* for something like this? You try hard not to look at me, much less come this close."

"I meant the waves…"

"I know what you *meant*." He studied her from underneath hooded eyes. "But I'm used to getting hurt on the way to learning something new."

Interesting statement from this man. So, he was accustomed to physical pain, and this made sense given his former career. No doubt she was dealing with a type A adrenaline junkie. She really could not relate, as she was entirely risk averse.

She reached for a Band-Aid and placed it on the part of his chin where he had the cut. Gently, she took the ice towel and held it to his wounded eye.

"Why do you do it? Why take this kind of punishment? After all your rodeo injuries, shouldn't you be slowing down? Staying away from another sport that could cause you injury? Why don't you take up golf instead?"

As she asked the question, she almost turned it inside and out and asked herself: *Why do you only see your self-worth as what you can accomplish in your career?*

They had the very opposite of careers, brainy versus physically taxing, but the commonalities were a bit unnerving. Apparently, they were both motivated to excel at what they did.

You don't want to take the new job offer because you doubt that you can do any good. You're not sure you can be the best at what you do.

"*Golf?* I'd have to kill myself first," he muttered.

"What's wrong with golf? It's a highly skilled and competitive sport. Not dangerous enough for you?"

"Even basketball is boring. I've been an adrenaline junkie from the time I was born. I'm not going to change my ways now."

This explained plenty, like why he'd been so eager to take the risk of harboring a baby without knowing whether or not the mother would ever return. He took risks as a rule, but he probably hadn't witnessed the situations she had. Problem being, she was a risk-averse person in a profession that, at least emotionally, was high stakes.

"Did you ever meet a risk you didn't want to take?"

Reaching for her hand, he lowered the ice towel, met her eyes and held her gaze.

"As a matter of fact…yes. I have."

So, he did see her as a risk. And she got it. They were so different. No two people this opposed should ever consider getting together, even for a little uncomplicated sex. Like ever.

Unfortunately, his touch sent heat spiraling through her, and she began to think of all those "opposites attract" sayings. Two similar polarized magnets repelled each other while opposite magnets were drawn together. Once attached, it was hard to separate them.

Maybe two opposites could fill each other's empty spaces.

And maybe you're just indulging in some wishful thinking.

Maribel caught the desire in his gaze and felt the electricity pulsating between them. Her thighs tightened, warmth between them spreading like honey.

No, I'm not going to do this. It isn't smart.

And God only knew she was nothing if not smart.

But there were a few things she'd come to learn about herself when it came to relationships. She had an automatic attraction to men like Dean, who were aloof, confident, grumpy and ambitious. Obviously, her attraction began with the fact these men were mostly unavailable. Thus safe.

She might not understand Dean's attraction to surfing or any sport that came with almost certain injury, but she admired his commitment. Naturally, she respected the need to be the very best at what you did. For Maribel, being the best had come down to understanding people's actions, and she'd been frustrated by never making any real progress. People were funny ever-changing creatures.

She reached over to the medicine cabinet to search for an anti-inflammatory, and her breast accidentally brushed against him. He drew in a sharp breath, which sounded far less like pain than frustration.

"Sorry." Her face flushed. "But I think you should take something for the pain."

He shook his head. "No pills."

"Why not?"

"I liked them too much."

"Have it your way." She hadn't found anything in the cabinet anyway. Now, she traced the puffiness around his eyelid. "Gosh, I think it's going to swell shut."

"Great." He opened his good eye. "Stop looking at me like that."

"Like what?"

"Like you're enjoying being this close to me."

She almost sucked in a breath, because he appeared to be enjoying it as much as she might be.

"You should talk," she huffed. "Want to take your hand off my behind?"

"No, I like holding you in place so I can know when another swing is coming."

"It was an *accident*." She removed his hand from her butt and raised it to her waist. "And what if I am enjoying being this close?"

"It's not a good idea."

His voice, that deep and gravelly drawl, made her nipples hard. He was right, damn it, and she knew it better than anyone. She didn't know him well enough, but what she did know was they were too different. Still, there was a tiny sliver of something very real about him. He felt familiar. Something… nonsensical pulled her to him. It was, she thought, maybe those empty spaces of hers.

"I know you're right, but I have been known to agree to bad ideas."

He quirked a brow. "Point taken."

Emboldened, Maribel nipped at his lower lip, earning a groan from him.

His gaze darkened. "That's hot."

Dean kissed her, taking over, his wicked tongue warm and firm. His hand dove under her T-shirt next, skimming bare skin, sliding up and down her spine, settling at the small of her back. She lost her head and rocked against him. That pulled an even rougher sound out of him, and his hands lowered to tighten on her hips.

He had a clean scent, like fresh pine and sandalwood. She'd taken leave of her senses, and no matter what else happened, she had to hold on to what she had. In the past, she'd learned her lesson every time she tried to stray from who she was at her core. She was solid, smart and didn't take risks as a rule.

Finally, she ended the madness and wrenched away from Dean, breaking the kiss.

"We should stop. Like you said, we're not a good idea. If I'm attracted to anything about you, it's your accent."

The corner of his lip pulled up in a smile. "*My* accent? You're the one with an accent."

"Right." She snorted. "Either way. You're annoying. I don't care for annoying."

"That makes two of us. You're frustrating. And I'm annoying. Together we're like a powder keg ready to explode and offend each other." The rest of his mouth joined the corner, and he smiled. Full tilt.

Something went still and tight inside.

Inexplicably, she couldn't help but return the smile.

Chapter Nine

Dean's sexy neighbor said she'd stick around for a while as if he couldn't be *trusted* to watch the baby with a swollen eye. Well, he'd handled a lot more after far worse injuries. A tiny baby and all those diaper tabs weren't going to fluster him. Even if it had become a little difficult to see through the one eye. He could take care of Brianna just fine.

And after that exchange with Maribel, he was ready to do a hell of a lot more. He'd love a chance to show her what he could do even *after* an injury. It wouldn't stop him from getting her naked and quite happy, that was for sure. But there was the matter of the baby, and he didn't like the idea of indulging in a basic fantasy while shirking his primary duties here. First things first. Whatever he'd done, all his life, he'd done it well and exceeded all expectations. For a high school dropout, he'd demonstrated over the years there was *nothing* he couldn't master if he applied himself.

Besides, in the way of distractions, there was the tropical storm headed their way. He hadn't shared with Maribel that the wave swells had crested higher and sooner than he'd expected, a possible reason for his injury. Other surfers had packed it up and moved on out. And he got it. Surfing during a tropical storm sounded slightly insane to anyone who wasn't an adrenaline junkie. If not for the possessed board nearly knocking him out cold, he might still be out there.

"You have nothing left to prove," his old manager had said. "You've had a great career, and there's no harm in packing it in now. Sure, you could come back after more rehab, but you're thirty-six. You can't risk life and limb forever. Get out there, buy some land, settle down with a good woman."

A good woman. Yeah, right. Dean told himself his trust issues with women had nothing to do with his money or success. The facts were he was broken in more ways than one.

"Sit down and take it easy," Maribel ordered. "I'm going to change the baby."

"If you need any help, just holler," he called after her.

She returned briefly, her nose wrinkled. "Holler?"

Yeah, these California folks were cute sometimes:

"Holler. Yell for me. Call me. Shout."

"Then why didn't you say *that*?" She went past him, holding Brianna, headed toward the bedroom.

Dean flipped on the TV in the living room on a low volume. No point in alarming the Californian who didn't even understand what *holler* meant. She was going to lose her mind if he even talked about the storm. But even though it was the season, facts were he'd even endured many a hurricane without incident. One only had to worry if the hurricane landed in your town. And each one, for decades, had switched course and left South Texas alone, as if even Mother Nature knew better than to mess with Texas.

In the kitchen, Dean opened his cabinet and helped himself to two shots of whiskey, which sometimes took the edge off these injuries. He listened to the weather updates, then grabbed his phone and settled on the couch to quickly type a text message to his real estate agent:

Can't make the meeting in Houston. Will have to reschedule for another time.

She'd arranged a meeting between him and the current owner to discuss the buyout. A moment later, she replied:

When?

Dean made up an excuse about the weather. He'd have to see how these units held up before making any offer. Truthfully, he hadn't decided yet whether he'd invest and wouldn't be forced to make a quick choice just because the cottages were in supposedly high demand. Even if he'd shown up for the scheduled vacation, the reasons he'd wanted to buy this place were gone now.

From the bedroom, he heard Maribel's soft voice as she spoke to Brianna.

"Oh, you like that, don't you? Aren't you cute? Yes, you are."

Brianna cooed.

Funny to hear her talking to the baby like he often did. Listening to their exchange brought on a smile that made his jaw wince, and he rubbed it. He'd caught himself smiling more than he had in months around Maribel. She brought that out of him with her cute and feisty take-no-prisoners attitude. With the way she tempted the hell out of him. It should be easier to fight this pull to her. She'd only been trying to help him after his injury, and yet for a moment, he'd wanted so much more than first aid.

But they were a bad idea, as they'd both expressed, and he would remember that. Temptation was good for the soul. Good to remind a man he was still alive when a woman could wake him up the way Maribel did. He just wasn't in the market for a relationship that would undoubtedly wind up a failure. More than anyone he'd ever met, he sensed that Maribel saw the brokenness inside of him. She wouldn't want to involve herself with the kind of man who had a history of being nomadic, moving from one home to another, even in his childhood.

Cell still in his hands, Dean fought his instinct, but he wanted to watch the reel again. The same reel everyone who cared about him told him to never watch again. He wanted to remember, but he also wanted to forget.

Letting go wasn't any easier than it had been to hang on.

Don't do it. It doesn't help and you know it.

Only makes things worse.

Not listening to his own sage advice, he brought up the YouTube app and went to the video he tended to watch over and over again.

He was on his last ride at the National Championship show in Colorado with the best scores in his category. Expected to win it all: the million-dollar purse, the status of being one of the best in the rodeo. Ever. A good place to retire. At the top.

He'd come out of the chute with promise, the announcers and audience excitedly egging him on. The crowd went wild as the bull did its best to buck Dean off. But he did his thing and stayed on two seconds… three…five seconds…then for reasons Dean would always question, he was thrown even before he got to his all-time best score.

Seven seconds. Seven seconds changed his life.

"Folks, don't know quite what happened there. Dean Hunter is a real pro, but this could well be a career-ending injury. Let's pray it isn't."

When he watched, it all came back to him. He saw himself lying on the ground and remembered how he'd stared up at the bright blue sky, not a thought in his head. Thoughts would come later. Thoughts along with deep regrets. With the bull chased off, the dispatched medical team was able to tend to him. For once, the announcers were right. Career-ending, indeed. He'd never get on the back of a bronco or bull again unless he wanted to face months of rehab. If he'd only listened to his manager, he could have gone out on top. But no, he needed one more event, one more buckle.

It wasn't *fair*. None of this was fair. He'd done everything right up to that moment. Hadn't taken unnecessary risks, hadn't become hooked on pills, saved money, given to charity, given to his foster parents for all their kindness to him and been good to his fans. But in seven seconds, he'd gone off his game when he lost his concentration. He still didn't know why, except that maybe his battered and bruised body was finally giving in.

From now on, he was free and clear of any personal commitments. He'd sail into the rest of his life responsible only to himself. It would be a comfortable retirement with the nest egg he'd managed to put aside from all the wins. He had plenty of money, enough to last him even if he did nothing else. No wife, no kids. Sweet freedom.

He could buy this row of cottages in Charming though he was no longer sure it would be such a great investment. Even with all his money, he was no Bill Gates. One serious category three hurricane landfall and bye-bye real estate investment. Sayonara vacation home. Maybe he should move to Australia. He could go anywhere in the world and start over. He'd already been all over the country, never staying too long in any one place. Now, there was no point to staying in Texas. He had the ranch, but other than his patch of land, the only thing left for him were memories pulling and grating on him like the exposed ends of raw and twitching nerves.

Like the time his mother got him back from a foster home and taken him to the beach. A beach in Corpus Christi just like the private one leading from these cottages.

"This is our future, Dean. You and me. Someday I'm going to own a house right on the beach. You'll have your own room, and we won't have to share one anymore."

He'd listened with rapt attention, the complete and utter devotion of an eight-year-old boy for his mother. But not long after, she'd found a new boyfriend and spent most of her time getting high. Inevitably, he wound up in foster care again with a family that, while kind, wasn't his. He was careful not to get too attached, because it was all so temporary. His mother would inevitably return and get him back, at least for a while.

Sometimes he feared that, like him, his mother had been a born thrill seeker. Always looking for the next adrenaline rush. In her case, she'd found it in abusing drugs and pills. It had always privately terrified him that he might wind up like her, with something in his DNA that made him weak. So he'd stayed away from mind-altering substances and been better for it.

He'd always wanted to save her, too, but had only been a kid without the right words to express that wish. With the benefit of maturity, he understood his words may never have made a difference anyway. Not to an addict. Still, he never got around to telling her that all he'd ever wanted was her. A place to call home with people actually related to him. People who wouldn't give him up. And though he'd loved his mother, she'd failed him time and again. He wasn't too naive not to also have a deep-rooted resentment of her. Loving someone and hating them at the same time was a confusing state of affairs.

Pulling himself out of his thoughts, Dean turned the TV to the local channel. This tropical storm wouldn't ever make national news, but the local weatherman was all over it. He pointed to his nifty graphics and maps showing the track of the storm. They expected several inches of rain in parts of Texas, along with strong winds. Nothing he hadn't been through many times before.

Maribel emerged from the bedroom holding Brianna in her arms and glanced at the screen. "Is this about the storm? What's going on?"

"You hear about the storm headed our way?" He pointed to the flat-screen.

"Yeah, but no big deal, right?"

"You'll want to prep for possibly losing electricity for a while, but this is the kind of storm where you hunker down and wait it out. No need to evacuate."

Outside, a light rain had begun to fall in the past few minutes. Deceptive. In no time at all, it might be sheets outside. He wondered if he should walk Maribel next door now or if she'd consider staying here with him.

"It's hard to believe since it's been so warm and sunny the past few days."

"Welcome to Texas. Conditions change as they will. Nothing to worry about."

"Oh my God, it just dawned on me that you were surfing *during* a tropical storm!"

"Not during. Before."

"You're a madman!"

"You have no idea." He went to each window to double-check that they were securely shut. He'd taken care of that this morning before he left for the beach.

Brushing by her on the way to the bedroom, he checked those windows, too. He'd go next door and do the same if she refused to stay with him.

"Listen. You should stay here until the storm passes since you're from California."

"*Excuse* me?" She stood in the frame of the door, clutching Brianna, a semi-outraged look on her face.

"What does my being from California have to do with it?"

"You know what I mean. You're not use to this kind of a storm. Stay here with me and feel safe."

"Right, because you're going to save me from a storm." If she'd had a free hand, he was sure it would have gone to her hip. "News flash—it *rains* in California. The song was wrong."

"Yeah, but I happen to know not like *this*." He gestured to the window. "The wind is going to whip around out there. It sounds far scarier than it actually is."

She shook her head and clutched Brianna tighter to her chest. "But…our cottages are linked. If mine floats out to sea, so will yours."

"That's precisely the kind of thing I'm talking about. We're not floating anywhere. This isn't a hurricane, and even in a hurricane or flood, not everything floats out to sea. The damages are primarily due to flooding, but we won't have to worry about that here. This one is just a bad storm."

"So, we should be okay." But just then thunder struck, loudly, and she startled. "That's okay. It just surprised me. It's only thunder."

The self-reassurance tugged at him. She was definitely sweet when she wanted to be.

And a few minutes later, the skies opened up.

He pointed to the couch. "You can relax, put up your feet. Read your book."

"While an epic storm is brewing outside? Who can concentrate? I need to stay *vigilant*."

He smiled. "Maribel, I'm glad you're staying here tonight."

"I didn't *say* that."

He went for the big guns, because he thought he finally understood her a little better. Like him, he would bet she never wanted to be the weak link. Used to solving problems, she probably hated the lack of control she had in this situation.

"Look, I'll feel better if you stay. I'm prepared. I've already been to the store to get supplies."

"Oh." That seemed to pop the sass right out of her balloon.

"I take it you haven't?"

"No. Well, if it would make *you* feel better, I'll stay. We need to think about Brianna after all. She's our first concern."

"Good. Thank you. You never know, we might lose power for a while. In fact, it's likely."

With that, he pulled out candles, matches and flashlights. The landlord had wisely left sandbags stored and accessible in case of flooding. Even if Dean doubted they'd be needed, it couldn't hurt to put them near the patio doors leading to the beach.

He'd take fewer risks with both Maribel and a baby in his care.

Outside, the torrential downpour and whistling wind created an eerie sound.

Thunder crashed like a cannonball. An explosion of sound and light flashed in the sky. And Dean was outside in this mess. With a black eye.

He was, interestingly, a lot like her, as if flipping a coin to see its other matching side. Whenever there'd been any kind of trouble at home, Maribel always wanted to help. When Jordan and Rafe had broken up so often as young lovers, she'd acted as intermediary. When her parents hit the roof after Max enlisted in the service, fear clouding their pride, she'd smoothed the way. "Pacificadora familiar," her mother called her affectionately. The family peacemaker. Maribel had always been fascinated by what made people behave the way they did. She could never stand by and just watch situations and relationships implode.

Unable to stand by helplessly any longer, Maribel made herself useful. She'd grown up as part of a family in which each member had an assignment, a chore, a duty. Her DNA wouldn't allow her to sit still. She'd already figured her part in all this. She would guard this baby with her life.

She set Brianna down in the bouncy seat next to her and heated water in pots on the stove so they'd have hot water for a while if the electricity went out.

When Dean walked inside the house, he was soaked, like he'd gone for a swim wearing clothes. He blinked water from his lashes, and his swollen eye looked even worse now.

He walked by her, leaving behind a squishy sound. "I'll change and be right with you."

"Don't rush. I'm… I'm perfectly fine."

She wanted to tell him she'd be okay, that she only wanted to help, not slow him down. Instead, she made herself useful by warming a bottle for Brianna. But the little angel had dozed off in the bouncy seat. Outside, the sky had darkened to the point it looked like midnight even though it was only dinnertime. Maribel didn't know what else to do but stand like a sentry in front of the baby.

Dean eventually rejoined her. He wore a new pair of jeans and this time, thankfully, a shirt.

He peered over Maribel's shoulder. "She'll obviously sleep through anything as long as it's not the middle of the night."

"She doesn't know what's happening. It's just another day to her."

Maribel was about to state her momentary envy for Brianna when the lights flickered and, with a loud pop, shut off. In the dark, Maribel automatically reached behind her for Dean, but he had her first. His arm wrapped around her waist and pulled her to him. The warmth and strength of this touch sent heat pulsating through her.

His breath was warm against her neck. "Hang on."

Then the light on his ever-present phone flashed on, and he took her hand and led them to the kitchen. Together, they lit candles using the matchbook and placed them around the room. There were two handheld flashlights, and he gave her one, taking the other.

Even so, in the darkness, the pulse of Dean's magnetism seemed to quadruple in energy.

"You're going to be safe, Maribel. I'll make sure of it. Even if we are strangers." He took her hand again, and the move felt more tender than protective. Genuine.

It didn't feel even slightly odd to lace her fingers through his. "You don't feel like a stranger anymore."

Apparently, the weight of the darkness had also given her courage, because she would have never said those words to him in the light of day.

"That's because we've been together so much in the short time we've known each other. It's been sort of an accelerated get-to-know-you through no fault of our own."

"Because of Brianna. I've been meaning to tell you… I'm glad you talked me into waiting to call the authorities. I think I was afraid."

"Understandable. Having been in your position, I might feel the same. It was a risk."

"No, I mean… I was worried I'd get too attached. I used to put distance between me and the people I tried to help. I pretended it didn't matter, because otherwise, it became too painful. I couldn't allow myself to be invested in the outcome."

"But that didn't work, did it? Because you were invested. You must have been very good at what you did."

Still holding her hand, he grabbed the carrier and walked them both back to the couch, where they sat knee to knee and next to Brianna, who was still sleeping. Maribel wondered if the storm was creating a kind of white noise, the dull sounds she'd heard could lull a baby to sleep. Her sister-in-law used to turn on the vacuum cleaner to keep her baby sleeping.

She and Dean were quiet for several minutes, shadows mixing with the ambient candlelight. This could be romantic if they weren't taking care of someone else's baby.

In the middle of a huge storm.

Chapter Ten

"Hey, Maribel."

The sudden sound of Dean's voice rising out of the absolute stillness in the room sent a jolt of surprise through her.

"This is a good time to tell me why you walked away from your career."

Of all the questions he might ask, she didn't expect this one. It was a question she didn't quite know how to answer. Truthfully, she was still in the middle of analyzing herself. It was hard to do, considering she couldn't very well be impartial. But for someone who liked to excel, she'd certainly gone into the wrong field. She should have gone into a field less dependent on human decisions.

She went for the raw and unvarnished truth.

"I told you, I had a better offer."

"Yeah, and…?"

"I think…honestly, I got tired of failing." She straightened. "For me, failure was never an option. I worked hard all my life. But no matter what I did, I couldn't seem to make a difference. I couldn't *help*."

"Something tells me that's not true."

"Patterns kept repeating, and I'd stand by and watch it happen. Over and over again."

"People are flawed in every way. And you were dealing with the worst of those situations. When a kid is involved who needs protection."

"You do understand."

"It's a no-win situation. You don't have control over the choices someone else makes for their life. You're simply there to rescue a child."

"That's what you're trying to do here, isn't it? From the beginning, you wanted to be the one to rescue Brianna. To protect her."

"Maybe. It's entirely possible that I'm still trying to fix something broken. I guess we have something in common, but went about it in different ways."

"I thought you were just trying to be difficult or that you had a problem with the system. I should have realized."

"Don't make me out to be a saint. I'm far from it. I just think people need second chances."

"That sounds like it's coming from a personal place."

"Thank you, Doctor." He snorted. "Have you been analyzing me this whole time?"

"No, not the *entire* time. And who told you I'm a doctor?"

"Your very proud brother."

She hesitated a beat. "I'm a PhD, and not too many people refer to us as doctors. It's not like I have an MD after my last name."

"But you *are* a doctor." By the dim light, she could see him stretch his long legs out next to her, and one of them bumped against her knee. "So, what's the verdict? Am I a narcissist? A masochist? Some other kind of chist?"

Something had made him bitter. Something or *someone* had given him a hero complex.

Stop it. You don't need to psychoanalyze everyone, Jordan's voice said in Maribel's head.

But it's fun, she answered imaginary Jordan.

It's a relationship killer.

She wasn't wrong.

If she was ever going to be in a successful relationship, she would have to trust a man. Stop analyzing him. Who he was, what he wanted, what his false belief was about himself.

But Dean *was* asking.

"I'm an amateur when it comes to analysis, but I *would* have said you're a masochist." She sent him a smirk. "Now, I think you've got a hero complex. You made it easy the moment you offered to take care of the baby. I saw who you really are even if I didn't quite understand why."

He chuckled. "How about you? How did you get into social services? What drew you into such a difficult profession?"

"Who said it's difficult?"

"Really?"

She sighed. "Why not? I'll tell you. Sure, it's not easy sometimes, but I've wanted to help children since I was a kid myself."

"That sounds like a long story."

"I'll make it short for you." The memory was sharp and painful, and Maribel always rushed through this. "Her name was Isabel, and she came to school in filthy and stained clothes."

"Foster kid?"

Maribel nodded. "She was in my class. A nice girl no one wanted to play with because she had dirty hair and clothes and sometimes smelled a little funny."

"I'd bet the ranch you played with the girl. Probably yelled at anyone, too, who was cruel to her. I can see it now. Little Maribel shaking her finger at everyone else."

She shrugged. "Maybe. I asked my mother why Isabel's parents sent her to school the way they did. We weren't rich, either, but we were always clean, our secondhand clothes mended. My mother took pride in our appearance."

"And?"

"My mother said, 'Some children don't have anyone who cares enough.'" Maribel's voice broke and she took a breath. "The point is, I firmly believe Isabel's case was an aberration. Most foster parents do their best, and they're not in it for the money. It's their mission."

Dean took her hand in his again, and this time he squeezed it, and his thumb caressed her palm. He didn't argue about family reunification and whether or not anyone in the system cared enough to offer help to the troubled mother. She considered this a small win on her part. Maybe she'd succeeded in showing him a different side.

The lights flickered, then came back long enough for her to catch Dean staring in her direction. Only when the lights came back did he drop her hand and look away, leaving her unable to decipher the look he'd been giving her. Yes, they were clearly both attracted to each other, given the bone-melting kisses. But he was right. It was best to stay platonic, because *he* was a bad idea. She could barely manage a regular relationship with a man and would never be able to handle something quite so…temporary.

In a flash, the lights were out again.

"It might be like this for a while." He stood and carried his flashlight to the kitchen. "These surges aren't good for refrigeration. We should eat everything we can before it goes bad."

"That sounds like a *terrible* idea."

"Speak for yourself. I'm starved." He rummaged through the freezer.

"Shouldn't you start with the refrigerator? You really shouldn't open the freezer. Things will stay cold the longest in there."

She had plenty of experience. Growing up, her family had a refrigerator that went on the fritz frequently. Her frugal parents bought used units cheaply, then Papi would try to fix whatever broke when it inevitably did. On the nights the refrigerator gave up the ghost, they'd haul some food into the freezer and the rest into portable coolers. Mami would cook everything that might spoil, and the entire family would eat together. Normally, they had a strict food budget, but on those nights, they feasted like kings and queens.

Looking back, it wasn't about saving food so much as it was about togetherness. Connection. Funny how the memories she cherished didn't involve fancy vacations or fundraising galas. Her favorite memories were of all the days they'd struggled early on, when she and Jordan shared hand-me-downs and her brothers did the same.

When Dean removed a familiar carton out of the freezer, Maribel was pulled from her memories.

She shined her flashlight on the items in Dean's hand. "Oh my God, is that *ice cream*?"

Dean held up a carton of Ben & Jerry's.

"You've been holding out on me!" She was at his elbow instantly, brushing up against his arm. "That's my favorite brand."

He slid her an easy smile, cast in shadows but still

maddeningly attractive. "So, we *do* have something else in common."

They had a lot more, because Dean had proven to be a resourceful man who'd probably grown up in much the same way she had. A high school dropout struggling to make a living. And now, he'd quit the rodeo, so the poor guy probably had no money, prospects or any idea of what to do with his future. As it happened, she sympathized, but at least she had an education. Her prospects were wide-open. For the first time since she'd arrived in Charming, it occurred to her that moving wasn't such a terrible thing. It didn't mean defeat, because there were many ways she could help people, and a little separation might not be a bad thing. She'd already gained perspective.

"What about the rest of the food? We still might be able to cook a few things in the warm water, but not everything. Do you have a propane fuel stove with you?"

"I rented a house with a kitchen. What would I be doing with that?" When he turned to rummage in the cabinets with his light, she couldn't see his face, but caught the incredulity in his tone.

"I thought, maybe… I mean, you're a cowboy. Resourceful. You don't carry those around with you just in case?"

"Where? In my wallet? No, Maribel. I would rather hike out into these woods around us and shoot my dinner, skin it, then roast and eat it by the fire I create by rubbing two sticks together," he said, heavy on the sarcasm.

"Well, now you're making it sound ridiculous."

He chuckled. "There's a whole lot you still don't know about cowboys."

"Like?"

"Well, first of all, we live in the twenty-first century like everyone else. Ranches even have running water and electricity."

"Of course, I know *that*. I watch *Yellowstone*."

"Bad example."

"I know what you mean. Those people are filthy rich."

"Except for the ranch hands."

"Right. Imagine what it's like working for someone who owns the land as far as the eye can see, and all you get is a little bunkhouse to share with all the other rowdy cowboys."

A beat of silence followed before Dean spoke. "You have something against rich people?" He didn't wait for her answer, but handed her a spoon. "We're sharing. Conserving on dirty dishes and using one bowl."

"Or we can just eat straight out of the carton. Let's be realistic. There are *two* of us. This won't last long."

"You're a girl after my own heart."

The statement shouldn't have made her heart race inexplicably, but it did anyway.

"And you're just saying that because you're forced to share."

"You may be right." He stuck his spoon in the carton and took a big helping. So big it was nearly falling off the spoon. "We're not standing on ceremony here. Help yourself, Rocky."

"Thank you, sir, I think I will."

Dean paid close attention, and nasty as it sounded outside, with the rain coming down in sheets and the wind whipping through the trees, he'd consulted his apps and his watch, gradually becoming increasingly certain they still weren't in any real danger. A relief because he felt increasingly responsible for Brianna. She wouldn't be here waiting out a storm if he hadn't talked Maribel into doing this his way.

The ice cream long gone, Dean and Maribel were now sitting on the floor on a blanket eating all the food he had left in the fridge. Cheese, milk and sliced turkey and roast beef, which Maribel had paired with crackers she found in the cupboard. Cold beer, too, or more like lukewarm by the time they got to it. The hours wore on, and other than waking twice for a diaper change and a bottle, Brianna wasn't much trouble.

For the first time since he'd become involved in this situation, the entire focus came off Brianna. At least it did for him. He was completely zeroed in on Maribel. Mesmerized. Touching her was, well, something he should have done earlier. Her amazingly soft skin begged to be touched again, and he didn't know if he could restrain himself much longer.

Surprising himself, he'd placed some of the candles around their blanket, giving them a subtly romantic touch.

"This is *much* nicer than I would have ever expected," she said.

"Good. You seem relaxed."

"I am, Cowboy. These calories don't count, either, because they're happening during a storm." She elbowed him and took another bite of cheese on a cracker.

He cocked his head, wondering why someone with a figure like Maribel's would be worried about that. "Tell me why."

"This night is special. No rules. I mean, anything could happen."

The way she said those words slid over him, and the teasing gaze in her eyes gave him plenty of ideas how best to use this time. A distraction. In one move, he reached for her waist and hauled her even closer. She didn't resist, leaning her head against his shoulder.

"What are you thinking?" He leaned in to whisper the words into her soft neck.

"Reading by flashlight?" She gave him a wicked grin, as if knowing the reaction she'd get from him.

He groaned and buried his face in her hair, gratified at the sigh that came out of her. "I don't want to sleep right now."

"That's not the only reason to read a book." She leaned forward and picked up the book she'd left for him. "How are you liking this one?"

"Actually, I have a few notes for you." He picked up his phone and scrolled.

"What do you mean *notes*?" Maribel turned to face him.

"Things the author got wrong about ranch life. You're not the only one who's clueless about cowboys."

"Yeah?"

"We don't all walk around with a rope around our neck, ready to steer some cattle." He smirked.

"Hmm." She traced his neck with her finger. "Correct. Go on."

"ATVs are becoming the norm. They're not as romantic as a horse, but that's the harsh cold reality. And sex in a stable? Let's just say, you wouldn't want to."

She batted her eyelashes. "Not even with a handsome stable boy who caught my eye?"

"All the hay. It gets in…places. Not a good idea." He shook his head.

Maribel laughed and lightly smacked his shoulder. "You're harshening my fictional world. Can't you just allow me a little escapism? That's half the fun."

"Okay, I get it. It's all about the image. Tall cowboy leaning against a fence, a look of concern on his face. They're about to raise the price of hay and that's going to complicate everything."

She waved a hand. "Um, no. Concern *because* he's about to lose the woman he loves to the local veterinarian."

"While leaning against a fence? Serves him right. He should be *doing* something about it."

Now Maribel threw back her head and laughed. And that sound. *Damn.* A full belly laugh, bawdy and wicked. Not at all girlish and sweet as he might have imagined.

"He will, once you open the pages of the book. Everything and anything it takes to get her back."

With that, she opened the book to the page he'd dog-eared and gave a disapproving sound "*This* is a no-no."

"Noted."

He held the light of his phone toward the book so she could read. There was no way he'd get any reading done with her sitting this close, between his legs, practically in his lap. Her back to him, she leaned against his chest, adjusting the book. He went ahead and pretended the fictional life of a struggling cowboy was of any concern to him right now, managing to read two entire sentences. After a few minutes, the reading, at least in his mind, just became an excuse to lay over each other. A reason to lower his head to her neck and brush his lips against her ear.

"I've read this sentence three times, and I still have no idea what I just read," Maribel said with a moan. "I can't concentrate."

"And I should save my battery." He lowered the phone, leaving them with only the ambient light of candles.

She dropped the book, then turned in his arms to face him. "What now?"

"I might have a few ideas."

Her gaze lowered to his lips, she softly brushed a kiss against him, ending by licking his lower lip. "There. That's *my* suggestion."

"Well, damn. It's about time."

Slowly, he reached to tug on a lock of her hair. Silky soft. Her eyes were shadowed with lust, and he couldn't actually remember the last time a woman had looked at him in quite this way. Like she understood him, like she could read him. Possibly never.

Gratifying, too, because he didn't want to be alone in this…whatever *this* was. This crazy idea about the two of them together. Hand on the nape of her neck, he pulled her close enough to share a breath. Her eyes were warm and fluid, showing him what he wanted to see. An invitation. When his gaze slipped to her lips, he knew he was in trouble here. Maribel was sexy and pretty. Real. Not at all stuck-up as he'd previously believed.

And she was one hell of a complication in his already upended life.

He kissed her deep, long and lingering. When her tongue met his, soft and tentative, he tugged her closer still. Took the kiss deeper. Wilder.

She pulled back, a bit out of breath. Her cheeks were pink, her breath ragged.

What in the hell just happened?

This whole getting lost in a single kiss was absolutely new territory for him. It was out of control like the very best rides of his life. She kissed *him again*. Her hands fisted his shirt. Dropping one hand to her hip, he didn't stop until they were plastered against each other. A raw and untethered thought nearly knocked the wind out of him. He didn't want to let go. She broke the kiss, her breath coming hard and ragged, her lips bruised. Her gaze lowered to his lips, and one finger gently traced his bottom lip.

He took her mouth again in a fierce kiss, releasing all the tension brewing between them. She responded with equal passion, her hands skimming under his shirt. He picked her up, moving them away from the candles, and settled both of them on the couch. She pushed him back and straddled his hips. Pulling off her top, she revealed a plunging black bra reminiscent of the bikini top she'd been wearing the first time he'd laid eyes on her.

He traced the edge of the bra cup with his fingers, then lowered the material and reached to take her into his mouth. She leaned forward to give him better access, moaning and bucking against him.

"You drive me crazy," he groaned, finally giving voice to his more basic thoughts.

"Right back at you."

She sank her teeth into his earlobe, and every inch of his body tightened and hardened.

"*You're* hot," she said, helping to remove his shirt. "Honestly, you're the best-looking cowboy I've ever seen in real life."

"And I have all my own teeth," he said, functioning on low brain wattage.

"You have so much more than that going for you."

"I own a horse," he confessed, stopping short of telling her he owned more than *one* horse.

"Now *that's* sexy."

He owned land in San Antonio. A ranch. Cattle. He might buy these cottages if they held up in a good Texas storm. But why ruin the moment? Rich cowboys were not the norm, so he told himself it was okay for him to allow her to be in the dark a little longer.

She kissed him over and over again, her tongue wicked, her hips undulating over him, making him hard as a rock. When she went for his jeans, he took control and rolled her under him, then stood beside her and unbuttoned the snap of his jeans.

And that was when he noticed.

One hand on his zipper, he stopped moving.

He pretty much stopped breathing.

"What's wrong? Hurry please."

"Um, Rocky?"

"Let's get a move on. I'm *so* ready." She reached, her fingers wiggling in the air between them.

But then her eyes must have followed his gaze. There, in the light of the flickering candle, Brianna's eyes were wide-open and fixed in their direction. She smiled, kicked her legs and blew a raspberry. Of course now would be the time she'd wake up when she'd slept on and off all day.

"Oh," Maribel squeaked.

"She's…not crying." He sat back down and ran a hand down his face. "But I don't feel right about this. She's watching us. It's like having an audience."

Then Brianna cooed and gave him the most adorable drooly crooked smile. Or she gave it to Maribel.

Either way, *his* night was ruined.

"We can't." Maribel sat up and leaned all her weight against him. "She needs a bottle and a diaper change."

More frustrated than he could ever recall, Dean stood.

"I'll get it."

Chapter Eleven

Maribel blinked awake sometime the next morning, realizing that she'd fallen asleep with Brianna on her chest. Also, she'd apparently fallen asleep on *Dean*. Even now, she melted into the soothing rise and fall of his chest as he slept. He'd held them both in his arms securely for hours. The last thing she remembered was rocking on the floor and swaying with Brianna until she finally fell asleep again in the wee hours of the morning. She'd sat on the couch next to Dean where he'd been dozing, literally too exhausted to walk the few feet into the bedroom and collapse.

Apparently, he'd gathered them both into his arms. The moment was strange and surreal. A baby in her arms, a man holding both of them. Somehow this all felt so…right.

She'd tried to postpone the inevitable, but she could almost feel her body hurtling toward him. Pulled by an attraction so big it took over logic. It took over her good sense. Her emotions were on the cusp of something new that she couldn't even name. Affection and tenderness for someone who seemed to understand her mixed with a kind of chemistry she'd never experienced before. Not on this level.

He understood her better than people she'd known for far longer. They were so much alike in some respects.

Brianna cooed and lifted her head, showing amazing neck control. Was that something new that her mother had missed, or had she been able to do that all along?

The sounds of heavy wind and thunder were gone, and in their place the sound of a light rain pattered against the windows. The big storm had passed.

A bit groggy, Maribel sat up with Brianna and cuddled her close, whispering to her. "I'll bet you want a bottle."

"I'll get it," said Dean in a sleep-filled and raspy voice.

She nearly jumped, because his eyes were still shut, and she'd spoken softly enough not to wake him. "I didn't realize you're awake."

"Just layin' here resting my eyes." He rose, his fingers brushing lightly over Maribel's arm, and walked to the kitchen.

Still wearing no shirt. *Gulp.*

Only then did Maribel realize she was *also* not wearing a shirt, just her black demi push-up bra, reminding her exactly where they'd left off last night. She'd been about to do something incredibly stupid and shortsighted. Caught up in her attraction for him, she'd let her brain go on hiatus. She couldn't do that again.

Laying Brianna on her back, Maribel quickly found her shirt and slipped it back on.

But memories of last night flooded her, making her face flush. Obviously, her inhibitions had lowered in the darkness. She'd forgotten herself. Dean was amazing, kissing her and touching her like a man who'd been waiting years for the chance. They'd both been stopped from going where they were clearly headed. Maybe it had been for the best. In the light of day, reason would prevail. She had no business sleeping with a man she'd known for such a short time, even if her intuition told her he could be trusted to take care of her.

But there really was no way of knowing for certain. The old doubt and fear crept back in, threading its way down her body, leaving her raw and vulnerable. Pure and unbridled instinct made her realize he had the power to hurt her far worse than anyone else ever had.

But maybe he won't.

She would trust herself, because she'd already proven her intuition about people was still solid. He was a good guy. Honest. The important thing was to slow this down, think a bit more, make sure sleeping together would be the right choice. She didn't usually operate on impulse, and every time she did, it was a mistake.

Dean returned, handing her the bottle, the hint of a scowl on his face as he took in her wrinkled shirt. She was equally disappointed.

"Still no electricity, so I ran it under hot water," he said, reaching for his own shirt and pulling it back on with sharp movements.

"All I hear is a light rain."

"I'm going outside to check." He went in the bedroom and emerged fully dressed, rain jacket included. "Be back in a bit. I'm going to check all these units and walk down to the beach."

"Okay." She walked him to the sliding door, amazed at his thoughtfulness. He would check on units that were, to her knowledge, still unoccupied. "But... Dean—"

She didn't know where to begin.

Are we going to talk about what almost happened, or are we just going to ignore this?

Are we going to make out some more?

When and where?

He turned, giving her a rare grin, and like he'd read her mind, he bent and pressed his forehead to hers. "Let's talk when I get back."

Maribel settled down and gave Brianna the bottle. When Dean was still gone a few minutes later, she checked outside and confirmed a temporary pause in the rain. She needed a change of clothes and possibly her cell. The one she hadn't checked in a week. After all this, she wanted more than ever to touch base with family.

Settling Brianna on her bed, Maribel quickly changed her clothes. She hadn't planned on showing Dean some of her best lingerie, but what a welcome coincidence. And there was more where that came from were he interested in continuing where they'd left off. She changed into the pink matching underwear set just in case.

Checking her cell, she found a few messages from home.

Mami: I know you're not checking your cell, and I'm trying not to bother you. But wait till you see what Rodolfo said to Imelda. He's back from the dead!

Her mother was referring to the telenovela they occasionally watched together. Mami from her house, Maribel from hers, texting each other the entire time. A running commentary on the extraordinary bad and over-the-top decisions made by main characters.

Maribel smiled as she texted back:

What a shocking development! By the way, there was a terrible storm here last night, but I'm fine.

Mami: Yes, we heard. Max told us everything. Since I can't talk to you, I call him every day. And stay away from that cowboy next door! You know vaqueros are no good.

So, Max had told them about Dean, but he likely hadn't told them about the baby. If so, they would be worried Maribel would do something to risk her position and career. They were proud of her and all she'd accomplished, the way she'd been giving back to their community. They didn't realize she had walked away from her job and was considering a career change. She'd been saving that little tidbit until she'd worked it out in her own head.

Maribel: But Papi was a vaquero when you met him.

Yep, her own father was a cowboy before he came to California on a visa and stayed when he met and married Mami. He hadn't seen a horse since.

Mami: Your papi is the exception to the rule.

The only exception? How convenient. Maribel didn't believe it for a second. Of course, she'd heard rumors that rodeo cowboys in particular were a smarmy, no-good lot for the most part. Traveling from town to town, loving the women and leaving them. Something about buckles, she couldn't exactly remember what now. They left their buckles behind?

But, as Dean pointed out, there was a whole lot she didn't know about cowboys.

And for the first time, she was willing to learn more. One thing about Dean? He was clearly honest and trustworthy. This meant more to her than anything. Most problems in a relationship could be fixed, but without honesty, nothing would work.

"You like him, Brianna, don't you?" Maribel pinched the baby's cheek, and Brianna smiled and kicked her legs. "I'll take that as a yes, and who can blame you?"

He'd offered to take care of a baby on his own and might still be doing it if Maribel hadn't let her guilt take over.

But she'd waited over a week for this moment, since the first time she'd seen him walking back from the beach, board under his arm, scowl on his face, hat tipped low on his head.

A long time ago, so her mother said, people used to *talk* to each other to discover who they were. Before the internet and Tinder. She, more than anyone else, had encouraged Maribel to take down her profile. Tinder was meant for someone less analytical than her. It had worked out to be true.

But now, curiosity won out.

She searched for Dean's name on Tinder and found nothing there. Then she did a deep dive of his name. If he'd been in the rodeo and wasn't lying about it, she'd find out for sure. He probably had social media pages where he was active. He certainly held his phone often enough. For all she knew, he'd been live-tweeting their entire relationship.

Met this girl. She's crazy.

Girl has weird ideas about cowboys.

Thankfully, it appeared Dean hadn't tweeted for five years, and then it had been to congratulate the runner-up in the Colorado National Championship. He'd been the winner.

Within seconds of her search, Maribel was assaulted with information.

He was pictured a few times with a beautiful blonde, a four-time rodeo queen. Both of them smiling at each other, they looked like matching bookends. She was no slouch in the Western world, either, a two-time finalist in the roping categories. It seemed Amanda Joulwan and Dean Hunter were as much alike as he and Maribel were different. She was stated to be "rodeo royalty," with her father being a former champion.

Linked articles announced their breakup a year ago.

There were also photos of him with fans: men, women and children. Funny, Dean didn't look even slightly grumpy in any of them. He was listed as one of the nation's top ten rodeo champs. Of all time. Top *ten*. She followed the internet trail and fell down a rabbit hole. Within minutes, she saw Dean was an expert in his field and very good at what he did.

But it was only when she found the YouTube video that everything inside Maribel stilled.

There were several, but the one with the most views was the "ride that ended it all." The date on the video was almost one year ago to the day. As with so many accidents, people couldn't turn away when the rider was thrown from his horse like a rag doll. It was Dean. *Dean*, who lay there on the ground for several minutes like a dead man while the action happened all around him.

Maribel couldn't look anymore. Tears formed in her eyes, clouding her vision, and she put the phone down.

It never happens that way, he'd said. *The rodeo quit me.*

It hadn't been his choice to quit. He'd been forced, according to an article, due to the injury.

A knock on the door sent her rushing to Dean while carrying Brianna, wondering why he didn't just let himself inside. She'd make him dinner tonight, definitely wouldn't burn it, and maybe they could even get Max and Ava to watch the baby for a few hours.

She threw the door open to find a young woman standing on the other side of it. Not the teenager she remembered from the bookstore. Not anyone Maribel recognized at all.

"Is Dean here?"

When the girl's eyes went to the baby, the love and longing in her eyes was like a gut punch.

Brianna's mother was back.

"You're her *mother*." Maribel's voice sounded distant and disengaged even to her own ears.

"Yeah, I'm Tammy Brown. With the storm and y'all being right on the beach, it seemed dangerous."

And so was leaving her on my doorstep.

What if Dean hadn't come along when he did?

For the first time, she felt immense gratitude that he'd come barreling inside her home, angry she would have forgotten her baby even for a minute. Because, of course, he was right to be angry with what he'd assumed to be true at the time. Truthfully, in his shoes, she would have done the same.

"We're okay," Maribel said. "The electricity went out, but that's all."

Tammy wore her dark and wavy hair in such an unkempt style it was practically covering half her face. She was dressed in blue jeans, Western boots and a black T-shirt with the emblem of a cowboy hat and a rope.

She chewed on her bottom lip. "Is she okay?"

"She's perfectly fine." *No thanks to you.* "We took care of her."

"You and Dean."

"*Excuse me?* You know Dean?"

"Well, he's kinda famous." She shrugged. "I recognized him."

Curls of confusion dotted through her mind, and Maribel tried to keep up. "Then… I'm sorry, you *meant* to leave the baby with Dean?"

She nodded. "Because I saw that you two were together and you made a cute couple. I knew he would have helped."

"We weren't… We're not a couple."

"I saw the way he looked at you. And then he brought your groceries inside, so I figured you were staying here together."

The realization hit Maribel all at once. Tammy had thought she was leaving the baby at *Dean's* doorstep.

Not hers.

They'd been standing in the doorway when the patter of rain resumed. "Please come in."

She clutched the baby tightly, still not sure she should hand Brianna over to her mother. Tammy sat on the couch, where not long ago, Dean, Maribel and the baby had slept together like a real family.

"You didn't leave enough formula or diapers," Maribel said, holding a squirming Brianna.

It was almost as if she were reaching for her mother, but Maribel told herself this couldn't be true.

"I'm sorry. I said I'd pay you back. Just tell me how much, but I just figured that Dean—"

"You misunderstood. We were strangers to each other when you left Brianna with me. Well, we *both thought* you left her with me. This is my cottage, and he has the one next door."

"Oh." Tammy wiped at her eyes with the heels of her hands. "Guess I got that wrong."

"You did."

"Can I…can I please hold her?"

Against her better judgment, Maribel handed the baby over to her mother. She thought of Dean when she did so. *Give the mother a chance. Believe in people.* And she would. Tammy took a seat on the couch with Brianna, and Maribel stood like a sentry in front of them. As if standing there could stop anything bad from happening to Brianna. As if standing there would import some kind of grown-up wisdom on this young mother.

Never do this again. Ask for help when you need it. Learn to find resources. Reach out.

The front door opened, and she turned to see Dean come barreling inside. "Maribel? Why did you—"

He almost comically came to a full stop.

"Oh my God, what happened to your eye?" Tammy said, her face contorted in an expression that approached horror.

"I'm fine. This is nothing." Dean briefly touched his eye, then lowered his hand and turned to Maribel with narrowed eyes.

"This is Tammy Brown. Brianna's mother. She actually meant to leave the baby to the both of us." Maribel cleared her throat. "Mostly to you. She thought we were together."

Dean's reaction was similar to Maribel's. His brow furrowed in confusion.

"I'm sorry, Mr. Hunter. I recognized you on the beach trying to surf. I read in *Rodeo Roundup* that you'd retired to learn how to surf. And then I saw you bring in the groceries for your, um…um…"

"Maribel," Dean said, filling the gap.

"Right," Tammy continued. "It makes sense you're trying to hide out a while. I...I just thought you two..."

"You must have missed the part where she slammed the door in my face."

"In all fairness—" Maribel began, but stopped when Dean held up his palm in a surrender gesture, then turned to Tammy.

"You're here to take your daughter back."

"I was worried when the storm came. Everything seems okay now, but it was a long night."

"Where have you been staying?" Dean and Maribel asked at the same time.

Tammy looked from one to the other as if she wondered who she should answer first, but there, just at the corner of her lips, Maribel noticed a tiny smirk.

"With a friend. My boyfriend kicked me out when he got tired of Brianna and how much money it costs to take care of her."

"And where is this boyfriend of yours?" Dean asked, his fists clenched to his side.

"I don't know." Tammy wouldn't look at Dean.

Maribel's brain worked quickly as she evaluated Tammy. Clearly, she was in trouble and needed resources. But the way she tenderly held Brianna gave no indication that she'd ever really wanted to leave her. She was just...out of options. Maribel looked for signs of substance abuse, but those couldn't always be seen clearly. For now, the girl did seem to be self-possessed and fairly articulate.

The moment Tammy mentioned the boyfriend, Dean began to pace the room like a panther. Every so often, he stopped to drag a hand through his hair and flash his famous scowl. Yeah, Maribel got it. The boyfriend was a douchebag, but what else was new in the world? He was probably too young and irresponsible to be a father, too. And though it wasn't an excuse, he was likely no more capable than Tammy to raise a baby when she didn't even have a home.

"Okay," Maribel said. "So, what's your plan now?"

Dean stopped pacing right in front of Tammy and waited as if he'd been the one to ask the question. Maribel would bet the girl still didn't have a plan, but at least she'd come back for her child. For that, she'd get a little credit.

"I'm... My friend said we can stay with her for a little while." She bounced Brianna on her knee. "Until we find a place of our own."

Well, it was a plan. Not a *good* one, but she had one.

"How old are you?" Dean spat out.

Maribel tried to send him a censuring look. They wouldn't get anywhere with his kind of an attitude. The words sounded more of a threat than a question.

"I'm nineteen," Tammy said.

"Where are your parents?" Maribel asked, knowing even as she did that not everyone had that luxury.

That gift. "Can they help? You and Brianna need a stable home."

"My mom died, and I never knew my father."

After a beat of silence, Maribel spoke. "There are programs that could offer you support and help."

"I don't *do* drugs," she said with a chin tilt. "Or drink."

"Good," Dean grunted.

"But I'm sure there are other programs we can look into to help you get on your feet."

"I don't need them." Tammy stood with Brianna. "We'll be okay now. My friend says we can stay there for a while."

"Then why didn't you take Brianna there with you in the first place?" Dean's tone was again gruff and irritated, and Maribel resisted elbowing him in the gut.

Dean surprised her. He demanded an explanation, which meant he wasn't as eager to forgive and forget as she'd thought he would be. But isn't this what Dean had wanted? For the mother to return and get her second chance? It was good to see he had second thoughts at the apparent lack of a real home.

"I had to make sure it would be okay and a safe place for us. Look, I'm sorry I bothered y'all. I really thought you wouldn't mind. And Mr. Hunter, I know you have all that—"

"It would have been nice to be asked." Dean cut her off. "Maribel wanted to call Child Protective

Services. You can't just leave a baby the way you did. It's called abandonment."

"But I *didn't* abandon her. I...I left you a note. It doesn't count." Her face twisted into the features Maribel recognized as defensive posturing.

She would fight for her baby because she viewed her as a possession. Familiar territory.

"This can't happen again, Tammy," Maribel said, purposely gentling her voice to be the opposite of Dean's. "Your baby needs you to stay strong. And if you can't be, you'll need to make some tough decisions."

"I *won't* give her up."

"You almost did," Dean said, and this time Maribel did nudge him. Hard.

He had the tact and diplomacy of a bull.

"Tammy, you don't have to give her up—"

Tammy tipped her chin. "I came back, and if you want, I'll pay you back for everything you spent."

"No need," Dean said, shaking his head. "How did you get here?"

"My friend dropped me off."

"You left her in a damn basket. Do you even have a car seat?" Dean roared.

"I don't have a car anymore. Too expensive. We take the bus."

Dean finally stopped pacing. "Look, why don't I take you two to get a quick bite to eat, and we can talk about it? Maribel, you stay here."

She blinked, shocked he was dismissing her so quickly.

Tammy stood. "Well, okay. I guess that would be all right."

Dean grabbed his keys. "The car seat is in my truck."

At this, Maribel jerked in surprise. "Hold on. Wait a second."

Dean turned to her expectantly.

This was all happening too quickly. After one week of caring for this baby, of bonding with her, they expected Maribel to simply walk away in the matter of a few minutes. She needed time to get used to the idea. She wanted to make sure they were going to a good home where Brianna wouldn't be neglected.

"It's raining," Maribel said.

"Roads are clear. I checked," said Dean.

Maribel desperately went through reasons why she could delay this. They should talk more. Figure things out. Make a viable plan for mother and baby. They clearly weren't ready to be on their own.

"Maybe you could stay a while. We have plenty of equipment you could take with you, but first… first, you need a plan."

"That's okay," Tammy said. "I've *got* a plan."

Not a good one, Maribel wanted to shout.

"Can I have her bottle, too?" Tammy said.

"That's another thing." Dean turned to her. "*One* bottle? Maribel and I have a system. You should fill them up and keep them in the refrigerator so there's always one ready."

If she even had a refrigerator.

"Okay," Tammy said. "Thanks a lot. Good idea."

"That's another good point," Maribel said, stalling for time. "We had a lot of donations. It will take time to get them together."

The caregiver in her couldn't just send these two on their merry way. Not without instructions and support.

"We can get those when we get back," Dean said.

Maribel grabbed his elbow and pulled him aside. "What are you *doing*?"

"Hey, don't give me that look. This is what you wanted. What we both wanted. Her mother came back for her. You don't have to worry about conflicting principles anymore."

"I'm more than my principles, *Dean*." She crossed her arms. "I think I've proven that."

"I know." He smiled wickedly. "A lot more than pure principles, which I discovered last night."

"Stop," she said, glancing behind him to Tammy, who was bouncing Brianna in her arms.

"Why? We had to stop last night, but there's no longer going to be a baby between us."

It was hard to imagine spending time with Dean with no baby involved. What would they talk about? They had almost nothing in common.

"Maybe…maybe last night wasn't a good idea."

"No?" He gave her the trademark smirk that told her he wasn't taking her all that seriously.

That might have been because of her own reaction to him. And he had a point. She'd practically inhaled him last night and would have gone to bed with him if not for Brianna waking up.

"You wanted her to come back the first night, and now she's here. It only took a week, and now you want her to stay?" The furrow between his brows deepened.

"No, I… I just think…"

"Maribel." Dean framed her face with his calloused hands. "We did something good here. Now, it's time to let them go and find their way. Don't worry, I'll have a long talk with her when I take her to breakfast."

"But…"

She could no longer even say that Tammy left the baby with Maribel, and so everything was up to her. It wasn't. She had to let go of this situation she'd never wanted in the first place. She had to let Brianna go. It was time.

"I'm going to take care of this part for us both. You and I were a team, and we did it. We got these two back together."

"We didn't do anything. They need help, Dean. Surely you see that. Staying with a friend is temporary. If she had *family*…"

"I'll talk to her. Have a little faith in people. Okay?"

She pulled on his arm. "I wish you would accept

that I know what I'm talking about. I went against my instincts, but maybe I was wrong. She's not in any shape to take care of herself, much less a baby. I feel like you're both shutting me out of a situation in which I'm the expert."

He met her gaze, his blue eyes softer than she'd ever seen them. "She's uncomfortable around you."

"What? Why?" She hooked a thumb to her chest. "I'm the one being nice to her. You're the rude one."

He chuckled. "*You're* the real threat."

"You shouldn't have told her I was going to call the police."

"Maybe not, but I think we both know you were right to consider it."

"Oh, finally! You admit it." She threw her palms up.

"I do." He scratched his chin and the beard stubble there. "But can you see how you're the bigger threat now? I'd lay odds it took you a while to hand the baby over."

Damn, he had her dialed. She crossed her arms and didn't speak.

"You got really attached to her baby. Don't deny it. Maribel, she believes you want her baby."

The thread of a memory came back to her, unwinding itself in her chaotic mind. A troubled mom resentful of a well-meaning foster mother stepping in to care for a newborn baby. A troubled mom viewing help as a threat. The child as possession. It was all too familiar. Tammy saw Maribel as a threat when she only wanted to help both her and Brianna. But the truth was she'd grown to love and care for Brianna. It was impossible not to love this precious child.

"I got attached. Didn't you?"

He cocked his head. "Not like *you* did."

"How can you say that? You…you held us in your arms all night long. I woke up with you *holding* us."

He smirked and tugged on a lock of her hair. "I was holding *you*. You happened to be holding the baby."

"Her name is *Brianna*," Maribel corrected, a pinch of irritation circling her rapidly tightening throat. "Not 'the baby.'"

My God. She could hardly breathe. And he was already distancing himself, better at this than she would ever be.

"Okay. I'm sorry." One finger slid across her cheek. "Go to the coffeehouse opening. I'll take care of this."

"We're ready," Tammy said, interrupting them.

"Don't you want to say something to Maribel first?" Dean's tone was stern and sounded like a literal scowl.

Tammy shifted Brianna on her hip and flashed a tight smile. "Oh, yeah. Sure. Thanks so much for helping Dean watch my baby. I appreciate it."

Thanks for helping *Dean?*

How about "Thank you for going against your instincts just to give me a chance?"

With a quick kiss on her cheek, Maribel let Dean strap Brianna into the car seat. Then she said goodbye to the baby she'd rocked, fed and loved…for a week.

Chapter Twelve

"We can talk freely now." Dean drove down the beachfront road. "I didn't want to say anything in front of Maribel."

The moment he'd walked in the room, he recognized Tammy. She had been a rodeo regular on the circuit getting way too friendly with some of the younger cowboys. He'd been out of the scene for a while, but she hadn't changed much.

"I don't want anything else from you," Tammy said. "Just wanted for you and your girlfriend to watch my baby. Because you have a lot more money than most people do, and don't try to deny it."

He ignored that. "Who's the father? Is it Anton?"

Anton was the kind of rodeo cowboy who wasn't

terribly discerning. And Dean had seen the two to-gether at least a couple of times.

She scoffed. "He wishes."

"Whoever he is, he needs to man up."

"Never mind. Just take us to eat breakfast and then leave us at the bus stop."

His gut burned because she was lying. "There's no friend in Charming, is there?"

"There is, but he's not interested in me *and* the baby. Don't worry, we'll find some place to spend the night. I have friends all over Texas."

"You expect me to just walk away from the two of you? To drop you off and wish y'all the best?"

"We're not your problem. You and Maribel go have your own baby. This one is mine." She looked behind her to the car seat where Brianna was cur-rently snoozing.

"She's beautiful. Congratulations."

"You can't have her."

He resisted the urge to sigh. "I don't want your baby. Neither does Maribel."

"She could have fooled me. She didn't want me to hold her. My own baby!"

Just as he'd suspected. "She got attached when you *abandoned* her. And she didn't immediately trust your judgment. Can you blame her?"

"I never intended *her* to watch Brianna, I thought you would. With a little help from your girlfriend."

"It was the toughest thing I've ever done, and I've been thrown from a horse and left for dead."

"Uh-huh. Serves you right. You shouldn't have dropped out of the rodeo. My daddy said you still had few good years left in you."

"Your daddy, huh? Is your mother even gone?"

She huffed. "I'm dead to her. She wanted me to go to college and stop following the rodeo."

Dean gripped the steering wheel so tight his knuckles went white. Seeing this situation from the other side wasn't what he'd expected. It made him wonder if his mother had given up a few of the times he'd wound up in foster care because she simply wanted a few months off, tired of being a parent. She'd never considered someone else might want him more and be far better equipped to raise him. Do better by him than she ever could.

Giving him up would have been the selfless act, and she never had. The realization was sobering. Even through all his underlying and quiet resentment of the way she'd never put him first, he'd never been on anyone's side but hers. A mistake. Maybe he'd been driven by an all-consuming love that in some ways had never made any logical sense. But it was time to rethink that.

For years, he'd taken care of his last foster parents, Jim and Maggie. He owed so much to them for taking him in, caring for him and maybe even loving him, only to be forced to let him go back into an uncertain situation simply because his mother had returned and been through all the steps to get him back. His biological mother, who held all the cards.

"You can't keep following the rodeo with a baby on your damn hip."

"Tell me about it. No one wants us." She looked out the window. "I'll figure something out."

No, *he* would. He had a chance to help. Get her back to her family. "Foster care can be temporary."

"That's where they take your baby away from you. I don't want that. I love her, believe it or not."

"She's a good baby, and of course you love her."

He believed Tammy loved Brianna, but she also didn't understand *how* to love her. Still too full of herself and her own needs, she wasn't ready to commit to the 24/7 dedication of a parent. Hell, even he wasn't ready at thirty-six. And facts were that some people were just not cut out to be parents. Ever.

For the first time in his life, pride took a back seat, and he could admit that had been his own mother. She'd been too young when she had him, too flighty and far too proud.

Reminded him of someone else.

Me, idiot.

Somehow, he had to convince Tammy to go back to her family. She had resources and help she simply wasn't utilizing out of her own stubborn pride.

"Maybe you needed a little time off. I get it. The whole experience was a lesson for me too, and I realize being a parent is life-changing, but it wouldn't be this hard if you had some help."

"Sure, because everybody thinks they know better than me. They all know what my baby needs, and they think I'm *clueless*."

Dean was so done with the attitude. "Did it ever occur to you that people want to help you and your baby out of pure kindness?"

"I don't think so. My parents wanted me to give her up for adoption. They don't want to help."

"Maybe because giving her up would be the selfless thing to do."

"Your mother didn't give *you* up."

It didn't surprise Dean that Tammy had heard about this. He'd kept much of it from the media, and only those folks closest to the circuit had the full story. It wasn't shame that kept him from talking about it, but a sense of privacy.

And I'm still trying to protect her, even after all this time.

He had to let that go, and finally admit his own mother had failed him. She would serve as a cautionary tale. Abandon your kid, and he might just wind up a high school dropout, choosing the riskiest career path he could find. Getting injured and physically worn out enough that he won't have anything left to give. To anyone.

"Well, maybe *she* didn't make the best choice."

With that, he pulled into the boardwalk headed to the Salty Dog, ready to get a meal in Tammy and then convince her to phone her parents.

* * *

"Welcome, everyone, to the grand opening of the Green Bean," Ava said to the crowd gathered outside.

With Max beside her, Ava cut the old-school red ribbon held across the front of the establishment. Then a dutiful applause from the residents and fellow business owners, and the doors were officially opened.

Cole and Valerie were ahead of Maribel in the line, their baby boy strapped in the carrier, like the one she'd borrowed from Stacy and Adam. She'd have to give that back now, far sooner than anticipated. She should be happy, but Maribel couldn't shake the feeling she'd forgotten something. The unnerving sensation had her checking that she had on her shoes and that they were matching. She checked three times for her wallet and glanced in the window to make sure no one could see her underwear through her thin cotton sundress.

She pulled her attention to all the ladies checking Cole out. He was a good-looking guy to begin with, another blond surfer type, but the baby was a chick magnet. He had the eye of all the single ladies, even if he and Valerie were sweetly holding hands like newlyweds.

Maribel pictured Brianna strapped to Dean's chest in the carrier. She'd thought her womb would explode when she'd caught him wearing the baby. How and *why* a man looked ten times more attractive holding a baby was a mystery she'd never solve.

Last night in the dark, he'd pulled her into his arms with such authority. His hungry kisses were beyond comparison. Dean and Maribel had been about to take their relationship to another level when Brianna woke up. It was for the best. She couldn't ignore their differences. Even after all they'd been through, he still believed a mother, *any* mother, was more capable of caring for her child than someone with more resources and responsibility.

She understood more than most how tough this life would be for Tammy, far more than she'd realized. The sleep disruptions. Walking the floor with them until they feel asleep. Still, handing Brianna over to her mother was one of the toughest things Maribel had ever done. The relief she should have felt had never come. She was still waiting for that overwhelming sense of peace to return with the knowledge she had her time back. Her life. Free, she could continue her plans to decompress before being forced to take the position and go home to start her new career.

She could do some good there too, because even if the problems would be different, children everywhere deserved support. The change would be welcome. This experience and this time had made her realize she couldn't go back to things the way they used to be. A change would have to come.

Ava gave everyone the tour, pointing out the huge industrial-sized roaster, the lever gently turning in a circle, roasting the beans right on the premises.

There were glass containers with freshly roasted beans and a giant espresso maker. The wood floors were polished, huge canvas sacks of beans near the front, and an old brick wall gave the place character. Over a year ago, Max had scouted the location in need of work and renovated it with a low-interest business loan. Maribel didn't understand how her brother worked his business magic, but it seemed everything he invested in worked. Even a coffee shop in a town where there were already two.

Then again, Max always said, "Nothing works unless you do."

He sent Ava a lovestruck look. "It was all Ava's idea. I just helped execute."

But to hear Ava tell it, none of her creativity would have worked without Max's practical business implementations. They were the perfect team, and a slice of pure envy slid through Maribel. Jordan and Rafe were also a good team. Her mother and father, too. People who had common beliefs made the best partners.

After the short tour, a line began to form in front of the glass display case filled with pastries. The printed menu behind the register was filled with quirky and original names for coffee blends: Milky Way, Major Tom, Almond Joe, Zebra Mocha and… *Leprechaun*? It must have Irish cream in it.

"Do y'all have a liquor license, too?" Maribel chuckled.

"No, but there's not much other than sugar in that

drink." Ava appeared at Maribel's elbow, pointing at the menu. "This was my hard-fought concession to Max's business plan. He insisted this was a huge demographic we couldn't ignore. Sweet and sugary coffee for the masses. But if you're like me, you just want a richly roasted cup of beans. We roast daily, and our blends are so smooth you don't even need to add milk or cream."

While Ava did sound like a coffee commercial, Maribel chose the Leprechaun because, c'mon, of course she did. Also, she was on vacation. She required all of the sugar.

"With extra cream, please," she said to the barista shamelessly.

At this point, it was too bad they didn't have their license, because she could use a little Irish liquor too. It had been that kind of a day.

"Is Dean watching the baby?" Ava said.

Maribel crossed her arms. "Her mother came back."

"Oh, good." Ava read Maribel's expression, because her eyes rounded in concern. "Isn't that what you wanted?"

The words stopped her short. She'd *wanted* the mother to have never abandoned Brianna in the first place. And when she had, Maribel wished she would have had the presence of mind to return the same day. Staying away for a week and returning only when a storm threatened the coast showed an appalling lack of judgment. Still, as Dean had reminded her, Tammy was the mother. Whether she deserved to be or not.

"I wanted her to come back the same day. She waited a week."

Maribel *should* swallow her bitterness and move on. Decompartmentalize as she'd always done in the past. But she might stew a little longer. She told herself it was because of Dean. She was mad at him for taking over and issuing orders. But if he managed to talk some sense into Tammy, Maribel reminded herself this could be a good thing.

Unfortunately, Maribel knew in her heart he wouldn't change a thing in a few minutes.

Ava followed her to a table. "Who was the mother? Anyone you know?"

"Someone Dean knew, or at least, she seemed to know *him*."

Ava quirked a brow. "Is he the father?"

Funny, once Maribel's mind might have gone there, and with her mistrust as a general rule, it was peculiar she hadn't. Somehow, for reasons she didn't quite understand, she trusted Dean. Maybe because from the beginning, they'd been in this together, and until last night, she hadn't been terribly invested in him. Now, she was.

"I definitely didn't get that impression. And she didn't claim it, either. She was young, as we suspected, and apparently recognized Dean from his rodeo days."

Maribel sipped from her Leprechaun, and the de-

licious sweet and minty flavor was almost enough
to cheer her.

"Rodeo days?" Ava's nose wrinkled.

"Apparently. You haven't heard of him? He must
have been really good."

"I'm ashamed to say, even as a fourth-generation
born-and-bred Texan, I've never followed the rodeo.
But those guys make a ton of money, so if he was
good, he might be loaded."

Not Dean. Nothing about him said he had money,
well, with the exception of his truck, which was
probably a rental. And even if it wasn't, Maribel
happened to know good deals could be had in secondhand vehicles. Her father never paid full price.

"I don't know what led the mother to believe he'd
be a good babysitter, but she thought he and I were
a couple. She figured he'd have help."

"What made her think that?" Ava said.

Maribel shrugged. "The way he looks at me or
something. That's what she said. Of course, she's
wrong."

"Interesting." Ava grinned.

"He was pretty good with the baby, I have to
admit."

"Debbie told me he's a good tipper," Valerie piped
in, overhearing their conversation. "But then, so are
a lot of folks, with or without money."

"Y'all talking about Dean?" Cole joined them,
holding his iced coffee. "He's a cool guy."

"Cool?" Maribel begged to differ. "He's a bit off-putting, isn't he?"

Valerie squinted. "Off-putting?"

"One word—grumpy," Maribel said.

"Hmm. Never saw that side of him," Cole said.

"Maybe only *you* saw that side." Valerie elbowed Maribel.

Both Ava and Valerie exchanged a knowing laugh.

"What's funny?" Cole grinned, but then was side-tracked when Max called him over. "Excuse me. I'll be right back."

Maribel watched as no fewer than three women checked out Cole's backside as he walked away.

"Apparently, men with babies are a hot and trendy thing now," Maribel said. "Do you see how much attention your husband is getting?"

"I think it's cute. And it does something for me, too, don't forget." She grinned wickedly as her eyes followed her husband and child.

"But speaking of Dean, I sensed quite a bit of tension between you two," Ava said. "Valerie, you should have seen them. Like an old married couple. You two couldn't stop bickering."

"He got on my bad side the moment we met."

"What did he do?" Valerie wanted to know.

"Well, he…he brought my groceries inside." Maribel realized how ridiculous it sounded, and the looks on Valerie's and Ava's faces confirmed this.

"What were they doing outside?" Ava cocked her head.

"They were outside maybe two minutes if that. It was…annoying."

Max appeared behind Ava, snaking his arm around her waist. "Maribel doesn't like to be wrong. About anything."

"Max, the baby's mother came back for her." Ava's natural cheerfulness made this sound like the wonderful thing it should be.

Max knew Maribel too well. His eyes squinted in concern. "Is that a good thing?"

"I don't know." It was the truth, and she wouldn't sugarcoat it. "We'll see."

"That sweet little baby deserves a stable home life and nothing less," Ava piped in. "I have to agree with you, Maribel. Whatever it takes."

"Thank you."

Now, if only Maribel could get Dean to understand.

After spending some time at the coffee shop, Maribel climbed in her sedan to drive back to the cottage. Her hands placed at the perfect two and ten o'clock position on the steering wheel, she didn't move. She didn't turn the key in the ignition.

This was all wrong. She had to take control or risk a child's life.

Whatever it takes.

Maribel thought of Brianna's little face, her sweet and drooly smile, so full of hope and innocence. Her mind fast-forwarded to her as a toddler and then as a preschooler, with an inattentive, young and possibly troubled mother. Bounced around from house to house and never having a true home. Her milestones would be delayed and, quite possibly, her health compromised. All because Maribel had failed to act on her behalf. For once, Maribel's heart and mind agreed.

There was nothing left to do now but make the call.

Chapter Thirteen

Dean spent two hours helping Tammy see the sense in his suggestion. "We'll go back so you and Brianna can say goodbye to Maribel. She deserves your thanks and appreciation for taking care of your baby. Then, I'll drive you home after you call your parents and tell them you're all right."

"They *know* I'm okay. I call them every few days, or they'd report me as missing and put up flyers everywhere."

"That's good. Your parents obviously care about you both."

"Will you talk to my dad? He would really like that."

"Absolutely."

Thirty minutes into breakfast, Dean had pressed

his advantage. He'd suggested that he might be able to make a call and smooth things over between Tammy and her parents. Not too surprisingly, Tammy did want to go back to her parents' home, but since she'd left them in anger, she didn't know how to mend their relationship. Since then, she and Brianna had lived at friends' houses, sometimes on the couch, sometimes in their own bedroom. Not ideal.

Her parents lived in a small suburb outside of Houston, where Tammy grew up, and deep down, even she realized this was a much better option for Brianna than perpetual couch surfing. She just needed help reconciling, and that was where Dean would help.

Considering her father was a fan, Dean could use his fame and finally do a good thing with it. He could pave the way for them and bring a family together. Brianna would do much better with an extended family surrounding and supporting her. Everything he'd read on single mothers agreed this was the ideal solution. It took a village to raise a child, and this time the village would be her biological family instead of overworked and underpaid foster parents. The way it should be if all other things were equal.

After breakfast, Dean drove them around town, showing off the boardwalk with the carnival rides and shops. They got out and walked around. More relaxed, Tammy handed Brianna over to him so she could eat the cotton candy he bought her. In so many ways, she was still a kid herself. He couldn't help but feel brotherly to her.

He stopped to play a game and won Brianna a stuffed animal. The smile in her eyes when he handed it to her hit him square in the chest, even if she immediately put the bear's ear in her mouth.

I got attached. Didn't you? Maribel had asked him.

This was a fact he didn't want to admit, even to himself. He felt a sense of protection over Brianna and couldn't just let Tammy walk away. Even Maribel would see the sense in his new plan. As soon as they got back, he'd share it with her. He considered texting her with an update, then remembered she had a wireless month thing going on. Crazy. Even so, he went ahead and texted in case she happened to be wondering where they were and why they were taking so much time. He'd missed the coffee shop opening, but Maribel would understand this was far more important.

We have a plan. Don't worry, Tammy and Brianna are going to have a stable home. Will be back soon and explain all. We need to talk, too. Let's finish what we started.

"Grandpa is going to be so impressed. Isn't he, Brianna?" Tammy said in a singsong voice the baby immediately responded to.

Brianna cooed and kicked her legs. She clearly

loved her mother. Dean could see that in the way her gaze followed her voice. He hoped Maribel had noticed that, too. And if she hadn't been too preoccupied and worried about Brianna, she might have noticed the baby was finally content. If Dean could get Tammy reunited with her family, a major goal would be achieved on all sides. Safe mother, safe baby.

For once, Dean could come full circle. He should have known it would happen here on the Gulf Coast, tied to so many memories of his mother. If he couldn't save her, then at least he'd save Tammy. More importantly, he'd save Brianna, who would grow up with the best of both worlds. Her mother and the support of her grandparents. An ideal situation.

They drove back to the cottages, and Dean held the passenger door open so Tammy could remove Brianna from the car seat.

"Are you sure you wouldn't rather stay in Maribel's cottage tonight? You could have the place to yourself."

"No, we'd rather stay with you. Wouldn't we, Brianna?" Holding her close, Tammy pressed a kiss against her forehead, and the baby smiled. "I sure want to be there when you call my father."

Dean headed toward his cottage, throwing a sideways glance at Maribel's, because he'd noticed her rental sedan parked nearby. Naturally by now, she'd be back from the grand opening, anxious for him to answer all her questions. Tonight, after getting

Tammy and Brianna settled, he'd go next door. Hell, maybe he'd sneak out and spend the night with Maribel.

By morning, this situation would look a lot better. He'd sensed Maribel's frustration at having to step aside and let Dean take over. She wouldn't be happy he'd shut her out, but it needed to be done. Once he explained everything, she'd understand why he'd wanted to take Tammy aside and, with his influence, convince her to do the right thing. Maribel wouldn't get anywhere when Tammy was automatically inclined to disagree with any of her suggestions. Maribel was a threat to her connection to Brianna.

Dean opened the door to the cottage he'd left unlocked and waited for Tammy to walk through first. He should have known something was terribly wrong when Tammy stopped just past the entrance and made a strange sound.

Dean followed her inside to find Maribel sitting on his couch with a police officer.

He drew in a sharp breath and told himself not to jump to any conclusions. With Maribel, he'd done enough of that until he realized he could trust her.

He was just getting ahead of himself and turned to Maribel with a question fully formed in his gaze.

"Were you that worried about us? We're fine. I sent you a text."

She didn't answer, but simply looked away, giving her full attention to the officer. This officer had inserted a sense of danger and doom, which was helpful to no one. She should be out on the streets writing speeding tickets and stopping armed robberies. *Nothing to see here*, he wanted to say out loud.

The officer stood. "I understand we have a little situation here."

No, no, this could *not* be happening. Maribel had not gone back on her word, not when Tammy had returned. Not when he'd figured out how to get her home to her parents without getting law enforcement involved.

"Everything is fine," Dean said through gritted teeth. "Thank you for coming, officer, but as you can see, I have it handled."

Officer Gonzalez ignored that. "I understand you abandoned your baby, miss?"

"No! I didn't." Tammy clutched the baby and the stuffed bear.

"That's ridiculous," Dean said, glaring at Maribel. "I was babysitting. That's all."

The officer blinked and shook her head, then turned to Maribel. "Ma'am? I don't appreciate you wasting my time here."

"You don't understand. Tammy has no home and nowhere to turn. She needs housing assistance and possibly a temporary shelter. Maybe even some counseling."

"Which doesn't exactly sound like an emergency," the officer stated with flat tone.

Dean didn't exactly blame her irritation at being

called. Family counseling was probably not why she'd signed up for this gig.

"Well, I...I must have misunderstood," Maribel stammered.

"I *have* a home. Dean was going to call my father. My father likes Dean." Tammy's voice shook and she sounded near tears.

All the snarky attitude was stripped from her. She was now simply a young and vulnerable woman who hadn't yet learned to stand up for herself. Who'd made one spur of the moment bad decision and would now pay for it.

"If you'd waited until we got back, I would have told you that." Dean spoke with what he hoped was a distinct edge to his voice.

Maribel had just about driven him to the brink. He had to walk away, soon, or say something he'd regret possibly forever.

She quirked a brow. "Parents? Tammy, you said you had no one."

"Dean convinced me I should call my parents. He's going to drive me back home. It was going to be tomorrow, but I want to go now."

Maribel flushed pink. "Sorry, officer, I didn't know this. It seems I've wasted your time. She said they had no home and were going to stay with a friend."

The officer sighed. "Well, looks like this is one domestic call I can leave with a sense of relief."

Still, she motioned for Tammy to step outside,

presumably so she could find out if she was speaking under any kind of duress. Maybe to learn whether the home she would return to today was safe for both her and Brianna. From the door, Dean watched as Tammy showed her ID to the officer, who took notes, nodding in places. He told himself this was logical and nothing he wouldn't do in the same position. As a sworn officer, she had to make sure all bases were covered.

But, damn, everything had changed in a matter of minutes. Maribel, who he thought understood, had shocked him.

He turned to the source of his utter frustration. "Why did you do this?"

"You took her away and didn't tell me what was happening."

"And you didn't trust me."

"With the story I got from Tammy, even you have to admit she needed help."

"I was taking care of this. I was going to take care of them both."

"I wish you'd shared your plan with me. You just walked away."

"Leaving you to have a little faith!"

"We still don't know if she's going back into a difficult situation with her parents."

"Which is none of your business."

"Dean, I care. I care about Brianna."

"And Tammy? Do you care what happens to her?"

She lowered her gaze. "Of course I do. She's Brianna's mother."

Maribel had blindsided him. She wasn't any different from all the people in his childhood, who hadn't cared about his opinions in the least. *Face it. You were fooled by a woman again.* Only this time it hit a lot closer to home because he'd thought they were on the same page. They'd connected even if he had yet to tell her everything. She might have understood him better if he'd simply opened up, but that was a moot point now. Too late.

"All I wanted to do was help!"

"You only wanted to help your way. You just can't see any other way, can you?"

Even after what they'd been through, caring for Brianna, she understood little but checks and balances. She didn't have any trust in the goodness of people. Maribel knew that Brianna hadn't been neglected. Sure, Tammy had made a mistake, and he'd been equally frustrated with her. But when he'd just gained ground, it had been ripped away from him. She'd likely never trust him again.

It reminded him of every time he thought he'd finally get to stay with his mother, because she was trying so hard to stay clean, when some well-meaning neighbor would intervene.

Don't worry, you'll get him back as soon as you show proof that you have an adequate living situation. Dean must have a proper bed and access to healthy food, one of their many social workers had said.

I'm doing the best I can, Dean's mother would argue. *Rent is so expensive, we have to stay with friends. It's not always possible for Dean to have his own bed. But he's fine. Just look at him! Doesn't he look healthy? And happy?*

The lady would glance at Dean, a smile on her face. It was as if she could read his mind and know he hadn't had a meal in a couple of days. Not that he would have ever admitted it. Whether or not he said so, he'd been removed from his mother for the umpteenth time and placed with kind parents who offered him his own bedroom. His own bed. Regular food and new clothes and shoes. Dean had marinated in guilt because he wanted all those things his mother couldn't provide. And rather than feel sorry for her, eventually all he had left was an underlying bitterness that she couldn't seem to get her act together.

But this wasn't a one-size-fits-all situation and the solution couldn't be, either.

"You know what your problem is, Maribel?" Dean raised his voice. "You don't have any faith in people. No faith at all. And it's really pretty sad."

"Dean, you don't know that you were sending her into a safe home situation."

"You didn't think I would check any of that out? At some point, you have to stop expecting the worst from people. Why does it take an expert to recognize a safe situation? She's a typical young adult, who doesn't appreciate what she had."

"I didn't know any of this because you shut me

out. The minute she came back, you stopped telling me anything."

He cocked his head. "Check your phone."

With that, he was out the door to confer with the officer and then drive Tammy home.

Maribel couldn't take in an even breath.

Everything had spiraled out of control so quickly.

You don't have any faith in people at all.

Dean's words echoed in her mind. They were particularly painful because they were so true. She hadn't wanted to believe it. A lack of faith in humanity was the reason she'd walked away from a career. It was the reason she doubted everything these days, even herself. She'd honestly believed she'd improved, but the only thing she'd accomplished was putting those feelings on the back burner. Coming here had been meant to be a respite, a time to think future decisions through carefully. Instead, she'd met a baby and a man who'd complicated her plans.

And now she was right back where she'd started with zero faith in people. Full circle. It was made all the worse now because she could see in Dean's eyes that he felt betrayed. They'd made an agreement, but when he'd shut her out, he'd given her little choice. She'd gone right back to what she knew. Familiar territory. Protect the child. Nothing could change the fact Tammy *had* abandoned her child. But if Maribel had known that Tammy had a family she could reconcile with, everything might have changed.

Dean was gone for hours. She waited for him in his cottage, eager to apologize, to help him understand why she'd made the choice she had. She had a right to make her case. But when he hadn't returned by late afternoon, Maribel made her way to her own cottage.

How had this happened? In one week, she fallen in love with a child who was not her own. She lacked the ability to compartmentalize her emotions, and maybe she'd been lying to herself all along. On a fundamental level, she understood that she couldn't actually be better for Brianna than her own mother. But her emotions weren't getting the message. She already missed the baby and wondered where she was, what she was doing. One week was all it took. One week!

When she couldn't focus on her book, suddenly not giving a dime whether or not the dog sitter and the actor wound up together, she dressed and walked down to the Salty Dog.

After the storm, the air was clear and even cooler than the previous week. Small puddles of water remained here and there, and she skipped over them. She should really treat herself to the carnival section of the boardwalk at some point. But as a child, she'd never been particularly fond of rides that made her dizzy. She'd actually never been a fan of dizzy anything. Maribel liked the certainty of a test when she knew exactly what to study beforehand. She could never understand why her classmates detested pop quizzes, either. The teacher had gone over the material last week. What was the big deal, anyway?

Life and love were a little more complicated. Too many variables. It was easier to see what other people were doing wrong, dissect and evaluate. Max, for instance, had never wanted to settle down until he met Ava. But his past had included continually going after the damsel-in-distress types who wanted security. Who wanted to be saved. A recipe for heartache. On their part, not his. People were strange. They behaved in unusual ways when emotions were inserted. She'd count herself among those people, because she couldn't stop thinking about Dean. And her thoughts had nothing to do with his looks.

Dean, with his unyielding attitude toward conquering a new sport. Dean, choosing to help a baby instead of turning her over to someone else. Dean, searching online for everything he didn't know and understanding far more than she'd expect from a high school dropout. He was as bright as people came. But he still wasn't being honest with her. Behind those amber eyes, there was something else, almost like a secret he held close. It didn't take a PhD to realize he was invested in Brianna's outcome more than most people might be.

Nothing can overcome love.

Those were some of the first words he'd ever said to her, and she would always remember them.

But maybe Brianna was all they had in common. The baby and a raging and undeniable attraction to each other. Dean scared her a little bit, if she was being honest. It wasn't that she didn't trust him, but since they'd started spending all their time together, Brianna had been between them. Loud, needy. Keeping everything…safe. Comfortable.

Maribel had rented this cottage to relax and unplug, not to have a man create chaos in her life with all the pheromones.

She opened the door to the Salty Dog. Inside, the night was cheery. You would have never thought there'd been a wicked storm last night. These Texans were used to all manner of natural disasters, and they were ready to overcome all. Everyone seemed to be celebrating something. After all, the holidays would arrive soon. But she was here to lick her wounds. When it came to a textbook, she was all-in, but she wasn't any good with people, apparently.

At least she faked it well enough to pass for an introvert who preferred books to people some days.

"Maribel!"

Valerie's grandmother, Patsy Villanueva, waved her over to the booth where she sat. Lois and Mr. Finch were on the other side, an empty space beside Patsy.

Patsy patted that space and Maribel scooted in to fill it.

"Hey, folks. Having a poetry meeting?"

All three were members of the Almost Dead Poets Society. Rumors ran rampant through town that Patsy was the romance writer of them all, with poems that verged on erotic. Maribel found it hilarious, but she probably wouldn't feel the same way if it were *her* grandmother. Or mother. Yikes.

"We're putting our heads together to see how we can save the bookstore," Mr. Finch said.

"Roy already volunteers his time there," Lois added, rubbing his shoulder. "But not many people come in."

"We do better in the summer months," Mr. Finch said. "Everyone comes in for the air-conditioning, and I always manage to sell them a book or two."

"Once Upon a Book? It's a wonderful little store," Maribel said, thinking of the colorful children's book section.

Had Brianna not been ripped out of her life in a matter of minutes, she'd have bought her a few books to take along.

"We thought maybe if we hosted poetry night every week," Patsy began. "But how many young people are interested in listening to a bunch of old geezers?"

Lois patted Patsy's hand. "More than you probably realize."

"But not enough," Mr. Finch said. "We need to figure something out. Twyla is struggling to keep it open. I'm sure you agree, dear, that a bookstore is not the proper place for yoga."

Maribel thought it was perfect. She usually bought a book each time she came inside, and the yoga instructor was paying a fee for using the space.

"Neither is coffee, but that works well for some places," Patsy said.

"If only Twyla was a man, she could enter the Mr. Charming contest and possibly win. That would be a nice help to the bookstore," Lois said.

"Have you forgotten, dear, that Valerie entered Mr. Charming not so long ago?" Mr. Finch said. "That's not a bad idea. Let's encourage her to enter."

"But Valerie didn't win," Patsy said. "Cole did."

"We should start up a collection," Lois said. "Save the bookstore."

Maribel decided then and there to make an anonymous donation to Once Upon a Book. Yes, print books weren't selling like they used to with the advent of e-readers and phones. Even Dean mostly read from his phone, and she hoped he'd tried reading the novel she'd given him. He'd bookmarked it, so she was encouraged.

Maribel couldn't imagine what her life would have been like without books. It was the one place she'd excelled.

"Have you talked to Ava yet?" Maribel asked.

All three got a gleam in their eyes.

"Ava!"

"How did we forget?"

"My memory isn't what it used to be," Patsy said.

"I take a supplement for that," Lois said, writing something on a napkin and sliding it over to Patsy.

"They're still officially newlyweds," Mr. Finch said. "It isn't that I haven't considered it, but I haven't wanted to bother her. What with the coffee shop opening. Those two have been busy, and before you know it, Ava will be pregnant."

Jordan was already pregnant. Ava would be next. Maribel had always figured with so many unwanted babies in the world that she would adopt. She'd already proven how much she could love a child who wasn't her own flesh and blood.

"Hey, folks." Debbie, their waitress, sidled up to the booth. "What can I get ya?"

Everyone ordered, and Maribel stayed to chat with the old folks. Every time the doors opened, however, she turned in hopeful anticipation. Dean could walk through those doors at any moment. He'd see her, come over to apologize for his brutish behavior and ask for her forgiveness.

I thought I was going to stop hoping for the impossible.

Apparently, Maribel hadn't given up yet.

The walk back to the cottages wasn't delightful. She tried to focus on the beautiful coastline, the seagulls foraging for food on the beach, the sound of the rolling waves. Instead, she thought every truck that passed by might be Dean. Every baby pushed in a stroller might be Brianna. Every baby crying in the distance was Brianna.

She was lost without a mission.

Next door, Dean's cottage was lit from inside, his truck parked nearby. She stood outside the door to her cottage, making just a little bit of noise, jangling her keys, hoping he'd hear her. But, no, she wasn't going to knock on his door and ask for forgiveness she didn't actually need.

Inside, she found her phone and dialed Jordan, who picked up on the second ring, laughing.

"Hey, there. How's life on the beach? What happened with the baby?"

Slowly, Maribel explained it all, hesitating on the part where she called the authorities even after the mother returned. Then, her surprise when she found out she'd been wrong, and the girl did have a support system in place.

Jordan groaned. "Well, you meant well. You always, *always* do."

"Then why do I always fall short?" The tears she'd done such a great job of holding back until now gathered in her throat like a sob.

"No one is perfect. I love Rafe more for his many flaws than his few perfections."

Maribel heard Rafe in the background. "Hey!"

Jordan giggled. "Well, it's true. And he loves my flaws, too. Don't you, babe?"

"Jordan, don't take this the wrong way, but could I have a conversation with my sister that doesn't include *Rafe*?"

"Sorry." There was some movement on the other end, and then the sounds of TV in the background faded. "I'm in the bedroom, and I'm listening."

Maribel curled up on the couch and looked out the sliding glass doors toward the beach.

Tonight, the moon was full, casting a shimmering glow.

"I love Rafe like a brother, but I'm pretty fed up with men at the moment."

"Understandable. Not long ago, I was right where you are."

"Dean must hate me now. And, well, maybe that's for the best."

"Not if you really like him. This is a forgivable offense. It shouldn't be a deal breaker. And if he won't forgive you, then it's best you know it now. Red flag!"

"I'm not sure I want to find out. He…he feels like a big risk to take. Maybe I should just leave it alone and consider him a vacation fling. A nice memory."

"What? And go back to Tinder and all the married men?"

"God, no. I'll just be alone. Maybe forever."

"Loving is a risk," Jordan said. "And you're going to need to take a chance on love at some point."

"I did take a chance," Maribel said, thinking of Brianna. "And I miss her."

Children came first. Everyone else came last.

Maribel believed in sunsets and books and anything that could be relied on. And if Dean wanted to believe in people, she wished him luck.

He'd be better off wishing on a star.

For her part, she'd be dreaming of Brianna tonight.

Chapter Fourteen

Dean was surly for a couple of reasons.

Number one, Maribel was in his head, and he couldn't shake her. He kept fixating on the look of confusion in her eyes when he'd gone against her. He'd lied, yes, a simple lie of omission. If not for his lie to protect Brianna, she and Tammy might be arriving in a police cruiser.

And wouldn't her parents have loved that.

"Your girlfriend is something else," Tammy had kept saying with utter disgust in her tone.

Even if he told her over and over again Maribel wasn't his girlfriend, she didn't seem to believe him.

Number two, and far worse than number one, he was starting to doubt that himself.

He wanted *something* from Maribel, that much

was certain, but he didn't think he wanted a future with her. She was the last woman he should involve himself with, someone who would likely question him and his decisions at every turn. Someone completely different from him with zero faith either in him or people in general. Someone who wouldn't forgive mistakes when he made plenty of them. He didn't mind being challenged, but this was different. She'd blindsided him, and he did not appreciate that. *Been there, done that.*

However.

She had a point.

He wouldn't send Tammy and Brianna back into a hostile environment. And he wouldn't just take Tammy's word that all was well on the homestead. He'd have to see this for himself.

Again, Maribel was in his head along with every social worker who'd ever been invested in his future. Home inspections to make sure Dean's mother had provided a stable home. He'd resented them as a young boy when he should have given those workers his undying gratitude. They'd put themselves between him and what he wanted because what he'd wanted wasn't good for him. They expected more than he even did for himself, and certainly more than his mother had tried to give him.

And Dean had to believe that Brianna would live in a safe place, because he'd come to love this little baby. And he wouldn't take Tammy's word for it. Not this time.

When he pulled up to the redbrick one-story home, Dean observed a middle-class neighborhood like the ones from the foster homes he'd grown up in. The neighborhood was safe, at least.

"You don't have to come inside," Tammy said. "But my dad would probably like to meet you."

Dean had already decided he'd do anything to ease this transition. He gently removed Brianna from the car seat. He held her close, kissing her silky cheek for possibly the last time.

"Yeah, I'd like to meet him, too. Always nice to meet a fan," Dean lied.

The last thing he wanted was any reminders of the rodeo and how he'd failed to leave on top as originally planned. Fans had a way of bringing the unvarnished truth front and center with their Monday morning quarterbacking, and for Dean, it felt too soon to have his failures tossed in his face. But he'd do this for Brianna.

He'd face his toughest critics and far worse. Even before they'd walked up the porch to ring the doorbell, the front door flew open.

A middle-aged woman that looked like Tammy might in a couple of decades stood in the door frame, her arms wide-open. "Brianna! Baby girl!"

"Hi, Mom," Tammy said, hooking a thumb to Dean. "Look who I met."

Juggling Brianna in his arms, Dean stuck out his hand. "Ma'am, it's good to meet you. I brought Tammy and Brianna home."

"Oh, thank you, Lord!" Without another word, she took Brianna from Dean and held her close. "I've missed you so much."

"Good grief, Mom, we were gone two months. You act like it's been two *years*."

"Tammy, I don't know what to say to you." She shook her head, then waved them both inside. "Your *father* is in the den."

"Oh, well, Dean was going to talk to him. And explain." Tammy shifted from one leg to another.

"*You* will talk to him." The mother's tone was no-nonsense as she pointed to a room down the hall.

Tammy skulked down the hallway.

"I'm sorry you got caught up in this," Tammy's mother said. "I'm Janet. And you are?"

"Dean Hunter. Ma'am, I won't bother you any longer. I can see that Tammy and Brianna are going to be okay."

"Did she give you another one of her sad stories? She was neglected as a child? We didn't want her to have this precious baby? All lies. Tammy lies when the truth would sound better. I'm ashamed to say that we spoiled her rotten. Well, her father did."

Dean scratched his jaw. "It's not for me to have an opinion either way."

"No, you've just been caught up in her web like so many others."

"Others?"

"Friends she's talked into letting her stay with them because she's tired of our rules. Mostly, she leaves the baby with us and has her fun before she comes back to be a mommy again. This last time, she decided to punish us. She knows how we adore this child."

Dean deeply regretted inserting himself into this situation. Now that he was assured Brianna had a safe place to call home, he could leave and never look back.

"I'm just glad to see she has a safe place with everything she needs." His glance to Brianna showed which *she* he referred to. "The baby was our biggest concern."

"We?"

"Me and my…my girlfriend." Why not? he thought, since it felt true.

Maribel, who he cared about and also hated a little bit. If she were standing here right now, she'd realize how wrong she'd been. But then again, she'd also see the sense in letting a third party be the one involved in this sticky situation. There was something to be said for objectivity.

Tough lesson to learn at this moment.

A minute later, Tammy's father came barreling down the hall, Tammy following. He stuck out his hand. "Dean Hunter, my lord, what a pleasure to meet you."

"The pleasure is all mine, sir."

The man lifted his fingers to his own eye, indicating Dean's bruised one. "Does this mean you're back to the rodeo?"

Dean chuckled. "No, sir. I'm officially done with the rodeo."

"Well, you went out on top. Don't let anyone tell you otherwise."

From beside her father, Tammy beamed, looking very much like a little girl who'd brought a present home for her father. And that was when Dean realized something so true that it might as well have been a bull running smack into his chest.

Maybe every child secretly wanted to please their parent, no matter what the reason.

Maybe now he could even forgive himself.

The drive back to Charming seemed to take forever. Dean told himself he'd done the right thing and that his anger was justified, but it still didn't sit right with him. He didn't love the way he'd left things with Maribel, with confusion and regret written all over her expressive face. He tried to understand she'd done what she could with the information she had, but facts were that Maribel did not have a whole lot of faith in people. She was jaded, and he understood that quite well. Welcome to the club. But all he had left to hang on to was hope. Hope for some kind of future after the rodeo. Hope he wouldn't take his adrenaline junkie personality into an uncertain future. Hope that he wouldn't ruin yet another relationship.

But hope wasn't a plan.

He'd had the chance for the first time in his life

to personally make a difference, and he'd come to truly care about Brianna. Even now, he missed her sweet little smile and the way she batted her hands in the air like a little boxer. Maribel might actually understand and forgive him if he shared his past.

But telling her his biggest secret, the one he kept close, meant she'd feel sorry for him. Sharing his roots and where he'd come from would only make her think less of him. A man like him didn't want the woman he craved to take to bed to think of him as a project. Someone to help and rescue. No. He didn't want the light in her eyes to change when she realized he'd come from a mother who'd abandoned him.

So, with plenty of time on his hands now, he supposed he should go back to his little cottage and luxuriate in being alone. Turn the game on and drink cold beers without the interruption of a crying baby or a woman. He could drive over to the Salty Dog and have a cold beer in the company of others but still be mostly alone. Just as he had been every summer. Just like he'd wanted in the first place. Or thought he wanted, anyway, until the day he'd witnessed Maribel struggling with the umbrella.

Once home, Dean noted no light on in Maribel's cottage. So, she'd left. Maybe for good, or maybe to visit her brother. The decision to ignore her was easier. What they'd had was over now. A time of unusual closeness due to Brianna, their main purpose and goal. But now the baby was gone. He and Maribel had nothing left in common. Nothing to build on because they'd had nothing but the baby.

He kicked off his boots and threw off his hat. He'd leave Maribel alone. With her superior analyzing brain, she'd eventually conclude his rescue syndrome had started somewhere in his childhood. Hell, he had no desire to spill his guts to her or anyone else. He'd lost interest in talking the moment she'd crawled into his lap that stormy night. What he wanted was more of that silky skin that had pressed against him last night. The soft and full mouth that had promised him all kinds of sensual fun.

If he wanted to chat, he'd call his former trainer. The man *never* shut up.

Instead, Dean dialed the real estate agent who'd found him this property.

She sounded ecstatic to hear from him. "Before you say anything, Texas is working on a better system for the Gulf Coast. Improving on the seawall and lots of other engineering projects. And a hurricane hasn't hit Charming in years."

"Missed us this time, too. The storm was fine. Everything held up." He'd like to check inside Maribel's cottage in the aftermath, but fat chance of that now. He wasn't letting her know about his interest in buying these cottages.

"So, are you making an offer? What are your thoughts?"

He leaned back on the couch and stretched out his

legs, crossing them at the ankles. "Make an offer, but lowball 'em."

There was a beat of silence. "I've already told you the price is under market."

"And I told you there must be a reason for that."

"Yes, they want to turn it over quickly. But they're not *desperate*, Dean."

"Good. And neither am I. I've never paid asking price for anything, and I'm not about to start now." He hung up.

Desperate for a certain woman, yes, he was. But did he need to own a row of cottages on the Gulf Coast? Not so much.

Dean spent a nearly sleepless night tossing and turning. The night before, he'd had the best sleep of his life, interestingly on a couch with both a woman and a baby pressing down on his chest.

He gave up on sleep as the morning warmed. Nothing to do but surf.

The weather app showed clear skies and calmer waves, so he likely wouldn't kill himself out there today. Good to know. He carried his board out, ready to enjoy the day minus one cranky baby and one sexy neighbor. Already ahead of the game. But there she was again, only a few feet ahead on their private beach, struggling with the umbrella. He heard curse words as she pushed, pulled and struggled against the wind fighting her efforts. If he explained she should push from the other side, she'd accuse him of mansplaining. He really couldn't win with her, could he?

He stalked over to the umbrella, set his board down and took matters into his own hands.

"Oh." Maribel seemed surprised to find him here when his hand covered her own. "I didn't see you there."

Within seconds, the umbrella was up. He bent to pick up his board.

"Dean, I know you're mad at me, but you didn't give me a chance to explain."

"You did what you had to do. I get it."

"No, I have a feeling you don't. There's a lot you don't know about me."

"And there's a lot you don't know about me."

She crossed her arms. "Fine. I'm willing to listen if you're ready to talk."

He didn't say a word, which only gave her the opening to keep talking. "With the information Tammy gave us, there was reason to be concerned."

"We agreed to handle this, and you blindsided me."

"Because you both shut me out!"

"I only tried to relieve you of the responsibility you never wanted in the first place. All along, we thought it was your responsibility, but it was mine. You're off the hook."

"Maybe it wasn't what I wanted to deal with, but I came to love that baby girl." She shook her head, and the ponytail she'd put it in bobbed up and down.

He could sense the frustration pouring out of her. It didn't escape him that it was similar to the confusing feelings rolling through him. The sense that he'd lost something he wasn't fully aware he'd had in the first place.

"You know what? In a way, I get it. Tammy didn't inspire a whole lot of confidence." He pointed to his chest. "But you could have had a little faith in me."

"That's not fair! I did have faith. I do have faith in you."

"You have a funny way of showing it." He picked the board up to emphasize his commitment to insanity.

He was all-in. That was how he rolled.

"You're not going out on the waves, are you?" She went hands on hips and oh, sweet Jesus, those hips. That soft skin.

"That's exactly what I'm doing."

"You still have a black eye!" she said, her voice scolding.

He snorted. "It's purple, a big improvement. And so what? It's a bruised eye."

"You won't be able to see as clearly."

"Clear enough."

"Why are you doing this to yourself?" she whispered.

"Doing *what*?" He stood his board in the sand with a thump, ready for this argument. "If I had a better offer, I'd rethink."

"Dean," she said, all the hot air seeming to leak out of her.

Her hands went down to her sides like she'd lost the argument and knew it well. It was good when someone recognized defeat. He appreciated that quality in an opponent.

Except he'd stopped thinking of her as an adversary the moment she'd agreed to help him with Brianna. They'd worked well together, or so he thought. Apparently, he'd been wrong.

"If we could just talk."

He stalked off to the waves without looking back. Why the hell did women always want to talk everything to death? It did no good at all. His foster mothers had been the same way.

It might help if you talk about it, one foster mother had said after she sat him down in front of freshly baked cookies.

He'd eat the cookies and forget the talking. There was no point. His mother had brought him back once again. *Just temporary*, she'd said. Until she got a new apartment after leaving her last loser boyfriend. She just needed a little more time to get a job, a good-paying one. But even then, he knew how long it would take her to get him back. No one seemed to understand his need to defend his mother.

Still, he'd done so whenever asked, and only later did he recognize just how pathetic he'd been to believe in her at all. He'd made excuses for her, forgiven bad behavior, and all for no logical reason. In the end, she hadn't deserved his loyalty or forgiveness. His love, maybe, because that was unconditional from a son to his mother. But when he got old enough, he should have made the distinction. He liked to think he would have, eventually, if she'd lived.

For the next few minutes, he hit the waves, or they hit him. Either way, a fight to the finish. He always considered it a major accomplishment when he stayed up for longer than thirty seconds. Coming up from the waves after one big fall, he found Maribel several yards away near the water's edge, her hand held cupped over her forehead as if looking out to sea. The moment she noticed him, she walked away, her swinging hips gyrating in a frustrated way.

Worrying her was not the worst use of his time, but when the next wave hit his bad knee, he decided to call it a day. He'd been out here long enough. Dripping water, he shook himself off and grabbed a towel, then walked toward the cottages. This meant passing by her. She stood as he came closer, lines of concern on her furrowed brow and puckered lips. Rather than assure her he was okay, rather than taking the other route and ignoring her, he chose to do what he'd wanted to do on the first day he saw her and nearly every day since.

With purposeful steps, he walked straight to her. Dropping his board before he got to her, he hauled her into his arms and kissed her. Hard. She made a little squeak in the back of her throat, which turned into a moan when his hands went to her behind, and he lifted her. Her legs wrapped around his waist, and she sank her fingers into his wet hair.

She broke the kiss, still in his arms, staring at his lips. "I just want—"

"No," he said and kissed her again.

She responded with equal passion, and he deepened the kiss, growing hard against her.

They both came up for air. "To talk about—"

"Later."

He squeezed her behind, slipping one finger under the bikini bottom, where he reached for and stroked a sensitive part of her anatomy.

He got the expected result when she gasped in pleasure.

"Okay. Later."

Dean didn't even feel his bum knee as he raced like a madman back to the cottages, leaving his board behind. He carried Maribel like she weighed only slightly more than a piece of paper.

"You can put me down, you know," she chuckled, holding on to his shoulders. "I'm not going anywhere."

"It's not that far."

"Don't be silly," she said as he jostled her in his arms. "I must weigh a lot."

"You weigh practically nothing."

He reached his cottage, and only then did he set her down to open the door. But he didn't let go of her hand until he realized maybe he was hanging on too tight. She wasn't going anywhere. She'd said so. They were doing this. No more thinking or skating around each other.

He closed the door and pushed her up against it, kissing her deeply again and again, stopping only to look in her eyes.

Jesus, she had a good face. Breathtaking. Gorgeous deep brown eyes, those incredible full lips. Her smile, when she gave it, was like a sunrise of unexpected colors and ribbons of pink and blue.

He pressed his forehead to hers and caught his own breath long enough to speak. "You're driving me crazy."

"Same, cowboy. Same."

"Glad I'm not alone in this." He reached for the nape of her neck and tugged her face up to meet his. For a while, I thought you hated me."

"Well, you're grumpy and annoying. But I just can't hate a man who's postponed his surfing time to care for a helpless baby."

"And it's hard for me to resist a woman who buries her principles to do the right thing."

"I...I haven't buried them. I just...put them in a suitcase."

He cocked his head and quirked a brow. "A suitcase."

"Because I'm on vacation." She batted her lashes.

Damn, she was adorable. And this was true. They were on vacation. Two consenting adults.

He refused to give it another thought.

Chapter Fifteen

Maribel realized two important things about Dean very quickly:

Bad knee, bruised eye or old injuries notwithstanding, he was strong and healthy. Like an ox. Or a...horse.

And lastly, he had a magic finger.

This morning, she'd tried to put yesterday behind her. Bury the guilt. Move on. Breakfast had been Dutch pancakes, and for once, her efforts were a resounding success. Delicious. Quite possibly, baking was the key. As long as the recipe called for an oven, exact measurements and a timer, she seemed to do fine.

She hadn't heard a sound from Dean's cabin all morning and wondered if he would ever speak to her again. Yeah, she got it. She'd screwed up. Again. Let go of all the progress she'd made while here and taken two giant steps back. She was still guilty of letting her past rule her future, but there were reasons for that. Reasons Dean didn't know or understand and, from his perspective, maybe he never would.

By late morning, she'd decided since the sun had burst through the clouds, she'd burst through her own fog. But the damn umbrella, her nemesis, had fought her again. Why did she have to fight for the simplest of things from life? Everything difficult, like her doctorate, for instance, had been easy for her. Higher learning and order. This was the key to life for her. The simpler things like setting up an umbrella and figuring out how to follow a recipe were like a foreign language.

Dean had come up on her out of the blue, stalking past her with his board. He unceremoniously dropped it, but rather than speak to her like a normal human being, he wrestled the umbrella and fixed her problem.

And, yes, she felt stupid, not a great place for her. Why had the words just dried up in her brain like they'd been baked in the sun?

She'd apologized, but he'd simply argued back, not listening. Typical. She considered giving up and going inside for some peace and quiet. Dean was too much of a distraction. But the thought occurred that maybe she should watch *him* for any more injuries requiring medical attention. He annoyed her to no end with his ridiculous alpha male need to conquer even if he had to hurt himself in the process.

But then he'd stalked toward her, and she'd stood, ready to talk. Or argue.

He'd grabbed her in such a possessive grip, and she'd discovered what she really wanted. What she'd wanted all along. It was him. *This.* She'd do herself a giant favor this time and ask no more questions. Just feel. Experience. Try mindfulness here, too. The rest of the world could stay away for now. Here, in this moment, they could get along again and forget they were two very different people and the most unlikely to ever wind up together.

Now, he and his amazing body hopped into the shower. For a moment, she had to stop and simply enjoy the sight of all the muscles she'd only been able to imagine until now. She'd seen him without a shirt, which was glorious, but this was…well, she didn't have a word for the beauty. No perfect words for the sheer masculinity of him. He held out his hand for her to follow him inside. She unhooked her top and lowered her bikini bottom. There was certainly no turning back now.

The hot spray of water hit her all at once, and Dean braced one arm against the wall on either side of her, pinning her there. His hot gaze grazed over her.

"Sweetheart, you are so beautiful."

He cocked his head and grinned, and a ridiculous and powerful surge of affection bypassed her brain and brushed against the soft underbelly of her heart.

Dangerous.

Dean gave her an easy, slow smile, and she responded by reaching for him again. Kissing him, the way she wanted to, without reservations. Without thought to what came next. It didn't matter anymore. His dark blond hair was wet and beard stubble covered his jaw and chin. She sank her fingers in that thick hair and pressed her body against his.

"This is what I've wanted since even before you clocked me," he said with nearly a guttural sound.

"I…didn't c-clock you," she said, panting. "It was an accident."

"Sure," he said, sinking his teeth into her earlobe.

"Honestly."

"Either way, I'm going to punish you now." He sent her a wicked smile. "Slowly."

She kissed him then, long and deep, filled with her burning lust for him.

Within seconds, their bodies were plastered against each other, mouths fused together, hip to hip. Heart to heart. He lifted her against the shower door, kissing her, squeezing her behind. She was on fire, molten heat spreading between her thighs.

He soaped up her nipple, then washed it off, and his mouth lowered to it. She went a little wild at his brazen touch, melting like a Popsicle outside during the summer anywhere in Texas.

"So soft," he said in a low and throaty tone, then went for the other nipple.

"Dean, do you—"

He held a finger to her lips. "Don't talk. Please."

"I was just going to say, I hope you have protection in here."

"Okay, good point." His hands lowered to her behind, tugging her close. "No, but we won't need it yet."

Then he continued to tease her and bring her to the edge simply using those magic fingers and his mouth.

And she found out they were pretty good together when they weren't arguing.

Later, they lay spent on his bed, covers tangled, limbs wrapped around each other.

She kissed his chest, then spoke softly. "Dean?"

"Hmm?"

"You're right. You are *really* good in the shower."

He chuckled. "You're no slouch yourself."

Maribel had something else to say. Something far more serious, which might ruin this moment, but she'd never been able to hide from complicated feelings. To take them out, dissect them, inspect them.

"I miss her," she said quietly.

"Me too." He tugged her close.

"It's so strange, you and me. We were basically coparenting before we even…you know."

"I know. And there's no one in the world I'd rather coparent with."

"Please understand. I just wanted to be sure she'd be safe."

"She is." He hesitated only a beat. "I'm sorry she lied to us, but I thought…if I got her alone, pressed her for the truth. And it worked. I met her parents and they're good people. Tammy is another story. She's a confused kid, but Brianna…she's going to be okay."

"Those poor grandparents. I can't imagine what would have happened if I'd called the police that first day."

"If not for the letter, I wouldn't have argued with you."

"You were right about me, Dean. I gave up on people. It hurt to hear the truth."

"I figure you had a good reason."

She couldn't talk about any of that now. It was worse than remembering the reason she'd wanted to help people in the first place.

"You must know of someone the system failed to save. That's why you're so intent on this, aren't you?"

"Yeah."

"Who was it?"

"Me, Maribel. It was me. I'm surprised you haven't figured it out. Remember, I'm the high school dropout."

"But I didn't—"

"Listen. I was the kid with a single mom who couldn't get her act together. She was a teenager when she had me, and when my grandmother died, she was on her own. The system protected me but did nothing to help her. I know she wanted me back and got me several times. About just as many times as she lost me. Eventually, I think she gave up. She must have believed that I was better off without her."

"I'm so sorry, babe." Instinctively and to offer comfort, she glided her hand up and down his biceps.

Though he managed to disguise his emotion, Maribel heard it in the strain of his voice. And it all made sense now that he'd been the forgotten foster kid. She should have seen it sooner, but she'd made a mistake in rushing to judgment. Her expectation would be for a foster child who'd obviously done as well as he had to have no issues. Maribel assumed she'd have to work for twenty years before she might see the results of some of her case files. But though he wasn't one of hers, Dean proved that the system worked.

"You probably would expect someone like me to be angry at my mother, and believe me, I was. For many years. But I was also loyal to her. Too loyal. Far more than she deserved. But that's the thing about unconditional love."

The thought of the little boy he'd been, waiting for his mother to return for him, filled Maribel with a painful ache.

"The system isn't perfect, but if we didn't have it in place, maybe you wouldn't be here today."

"I know people have the best intentions. But by the time I turned thirteen, my mother had died of an overdose. Honestly, I can't help but think if I'd been around, I could have called the ambulance for her. They might have been able to revive her. I was told enough to help, in other words. To save her."

"That wasn't your job. Surely you see that now."

"Yeah, of course, I do. But there's some small part of me that wanted to rescue her, that wanted to be the one reason she'd quit abusing for good. And I didn't have the chance. I loved her, and losing her was like...like someone turned off the sun."

And there it was. The painful tightness of his voice. He'd been devastated. He still hurt from the abandonment just as every child did. Every courtroom in the country believed a child belonged with his biological parents, and this was done whenever it was possible. But the parents had to want it more than anyone else. They had to fight.

"Did you have decent foster parents?"

"Quite a few who were okay. Good people. They just weren't *my* family, and I knew it."

Maribel reached for his hand and squeezed it. "She kept coming back for you."

"How did you guess?"

"Your loyalty, and this is who you are. You obviously never give up on people when they need you. And she needed you."

But it wasn't Dean's job to be the parent, and she'd bet in many ways he had been.

She took his big hand and threaded his fingers between hers. "She wanted you."

"Not enough to give up using."

Sometime during the night, Maribel reached for the spot where Dean had been lying next to her. The spot he'd kept warm and which smelled delightfully like him. Leather and musk. But he wasn't there, and she sat up, opening one eye.

Then she saw him, sitting on the chair in the corner of the room completely naked and reading one of her books by the light of his phone. If there was anything sexier than a man wearing a baby, it had to be a naked man reading a book.

"Can't sleep again?" she mumbled.

"I'm fine. Go back to sleep, sweetheart."

Hmm. *Sweetheart.* Once, she would have mimed throwing up if a guy called her that, but she rather loved the sound of that old-fashioned term of endearment coming out of his lips in his sexy drawl.

"No."

"No?" He grinned, setting the book down. "Getting bossy again? You love to argue, don't you?"

It was sweet that he hadn't left the room to read, like he didn't want to leave her alone. And while she could wear him out, if she wanted to, the truth was he'd worn *her* out. Their lovemaking had been nothing short of wall-banging sex. Sweaty, raw and... unexpected. Dean made her feel like a woman and also let her take control.

"Nah." She went up on her elbow. "I want you to cuddle with me."

He quirked a brow. "But how likely is that to put me to sleep?"

"I promise to behave myself."

"That's what I was afraid of."

Still, he crawled back into bed beside her, tucking her back to his front. He felt so good, his warm, strong arms circling her. Those arms were cultivated by a man who obviously loved to push his body to the brink of its limits. Judging by last night, too, in (ahem) *everything* he did.

"Um, Dean?"

"Don't let me keep you up. Go ahead, sleep." He kissed the nape of her neck, causing tingles to spread. "I'll hold you."

"I will, after I…tell you something."

He went still, as if he expected bad news. "Yeah? Go ahead."

"I haven't been totally honest with you, and you were with me. You deserve the full story. My…story."

He deserved to know why she'd left the career that had once meant so much to her.

"I screwed up. A few months ago, there was a case, my toughest one. You know, sometimes I'm sent out to domestic calls when there's a family member who is obviously mentally ill. And I feel so helpless. It's overwhelming. I used to think I could help, that with my incredible knowledge of the human condition, I'd solve problems. Needless to say, people are far too complicated and so is the human heart. But when there's a child involved, dysfunction is dangerous."

He nodded and waited, not prodding her, simply slid his warm hand up and down her back.

"I used to believe in people. Until a child was

taken to the hospital for dehydration. I couldn't afford to trust anyone. Not when it comes to a child."

"Listen, Maribel…"

A sob lodged in her throat, and Maribel's eyes burned with hot tears. "I didn't want that to happen, but it did. If I can't help, if I can't be the best, I wanted out. And after, I couldn't seem to change until Brianna came along. Until you forced me to take a chance."

"You wanted to do the right thing, and I don't fault you for that. Listen, when I see a bull coming at me, there's only one thing to do—get the hell out of his way. I'm not going to talk to the bull, help him see reason. A bull is a bull. An addict is an addict. You're dealing with the addiction, not the person you love."

He surprised her again with his knowledge and understanding. Certainly not what she'd expected.

"You're pretty wise. How do you know all this?"

"Went to an Al-Anon meeting or two when I was fourteen. And I've read a lot, trying to understand."

"The thing of it is, I almost shirked my responsibilities. I almost walked away from the baby."

Even if it was logical to her ordered brain, shame filled her because she'd separated all emotion from the situation.

"It makes sense that you would. But here's the thing. You *didn't*." He rubbed her back in slow even strokes. "Go to sleep now, sweetheart."

She decided not to let him know she'd done what she had to because she didn't trust *him* to care for the baby. Only because he'd forced her into a corner. She'd been so wrong about this cowboy who loved and took care of a baby. Eventually, she fell back to sleep, memories of her time with Brianna lulling her until rays of sun filtered through the blinds.

Maribel opened one eye and then the other. Dean wasn't beside her, but was sitting on the chair, the book dropped to the floor beside him. He was sound asleep, stretched out on the chair. Briefly, she considered waking him up the happy way, but he needed his sleep. Poor guy. For a moment, she took him in, his mussed hair falling over one eye. She pictured the boy who'd been separated from his mother, and her heart squeezed at the young man who'd been left behind. The young man who wanted to rescue his mother but failed.

From her training, she understood abandonment created a false belief that everyone would leave at some point and no one could be trusted to stay. Attachments were brief and transient. This made sense for a rodeo cowboy. Some strove for achievement, hoping to eventually be worthy of love. This was probably how he'd wound up on the rodeo circuit, earning buckles and the kind of temporary associations with women that went along with the lifestyle. No need to fear abandonment when you left first. He also had other common personality traits, such as his adaptability, loyalty and protection.

And he has the flaws, too. Like resentment, anger and occasionally withdrawing.

Everything in her screamed that Dean was a dangerous person to allow herself to care about. He had deep wounds, ones which would affect his ability to be a loving partner to anyone. And there was the fact they were both here temporarily, both a bit adrift in their careers and future plans. At least she had a possible plan in the works even if she wasn't thrilled by the prospect of listening to privileged kids go on about their problems with overbearing parents and slipping grades. It would be a change, and maybe she could do some good. The risks to her own sense of peace would be lower.

Maribel showered and dressed. While she waited for Dean to wake up, she made coffee and began one of her many attempts to cook a traditional breakfast. One that didn't involve opening up a box and adding milk. Her plans while on vacation had been, among unplugging and reading, to teach herself how to cook. It had been years of eating out or eating at her mother's, who thankfully loved to cook. But she was a grown-up and embarrassed to still rely on her mother for home-cooked meals. The baby had thrown a wrench in her plans to become the next Julia Child, or more likely, Pioneer Woman, but she couldn't let her plans die. She still had another week in Charming.

Cooking, according to Mami, was all about the effort, following directions and presentation. Her entire adult life had been about those three things, so she should do all right. She was, if nothing else, incredibly book smart. Maribel pulled out the recipe book she'd bought at Once Upon a Book and turned to the pancake section. Start small, grow slowly. Begin with the simple things, the cooking experts advised.

Propping the open page against the coffeemaker, she pulled out the ingredients she'd bought at the grocery store. A sense of peace fell over her as she measured, folded vanilla, butter and milk into the flour and added fresh blueberries with tiny sprigs of mint. The butter sizzled in the pan, and she added a spoonful of batter and watched as the bubbles formed.

Cooking accomplished something else in that it allowed her mind to wander, and she stopped thinking about whether or not she and Dean were a great idea.

"Hey." Dean came up behind her, wrapping his arms around her waist, lowering his head to her shoulder.

"Good morning." She dropped the spatula and turned in his arms. "I hope you finally got some sleep."

"You were right. There's something soothing about reading a book."

"And it has to be light and humorous before bedtime." She tweaked his chin, the stubble rough against the pads of her fingers.

"I will say I'm getting some interesting ideas from this *particular* book." He sent her another one of his slow and easy smiles.

So much better than all the scowling.

"I didn't think I'd ever see you smile." Something pulled low in her belly, and heat and desire spread.

He reached over her and flipped the pancake. Only then did she noticed it had been burning.

"Oh, dang it. That was breakfast."

"Looks delicious."

"Don't you mean *looked*, as in the past tense?" Maribel scowled. "Now I'll have to start over. I'll make another one."

He took her hand and led her to the bedroom. "Later. I want to try something I read about on page one hundred."

Chapter Sixteen

From the moment Maribel first sparred with Dean, she'd sensed something far deeper to him. Far more than the smoldering golden boy looks. Something underlying, mysterious and enigmatic. In addition to his being irritating, condescending and annoying, that is. When he'd told her his story, something cracked wide-open inside her. She'd now witnessed the other side, a foster kid grown up, making his way in the world. Succeeding. He'd proven that her life's work had made a difference to at least one child and possibly many more. It was a gift he didn't know he'd given her. He was a child who'd lived and succeeded.

Now it would remain to be seen if he was a man who could have a healthy nondysfunctional relationship with a woman. Whoa. Where had that come from? She wasn't exactly the queen of relationships herself. And she didn't want anything more than the time they'd have together here in this little cottage by the sea. A wonderful memory and nothing more. She was going back to California, and…well, she had no idea where he was going or if he even knew.

But, yes, something more would be nice, though she wondered what it would look like in everyday life. In life after vacation.

Dean walked out of the bathroom smiling, towel-drying his hair. "Want to do our thing today? You read while I surf?"

"Is that our thing?" A smile came over her lips. *We have a thing.*

"Yeah, it is. Among others." He lowered his head to the crook of her neck, his warm lips brushing against her skin.

A tingle went through her along with an all-body buzz. A tingle! At one time, Maribel would have told anyone who would listen to her that those tingles didn't exist, they were merely a figment of people's imaginations. A good touch in the romance novels she devoured. Deep down, *she* understood attraction was a chemical reaction. Her dopamine levels were at an all-time high around Dean. Science.

This was why she turned giddy around him. But the rest of it, the way he made her laugh, the way he seemed determined to be the best at everything he did, even if it meant injury, well…that part was different. She hadn't really expected for it to make *sense* to feel this way about someone like him. She admired him and respected him and maybe even loved him a little bit.

"We have quite a few things. And a lot more in common than you would think." He continued holding up one finger and then another. "Beach. Brianna. Books. The three Bs."

"Dean, am I crazy, or is this… Are we…" She couldn't even complete the sentence.

This emotion, this feeling coursing through her was so rare she didn't have a name for it yet. Being around him was addictive. So addictive she'd somehow accidentally on purpose put all her reservations about their differences aside.

Loving is a risk, Jordan said. *And you're going to have to take a chance on love at some point.*

"Yes," he said, completing her thought.

"Yes, what?" she chuckled.

"We started something here." He pressed his forehead to hers. "And I don't want to hear about dopamine and pheromones, Doctor. *I'm* a romantic."

"You are constantly surprising me."

"I plan to keep on doing that." He slapped her behind on his way to the front door. "I'll see you out there, Rocky. Bring a book for me."

"You're going to *read*?"

Was it strange that this was nearly the same thing as asking her to be his girlfriend?

"I'll take a break and sit with you." He turned and pointed to her. "Read a bit. Or make out with you."

"Either way."

He winked and was out the door.

Maribel changed back into her black two-piece swimsuit and gathered her towel, books and umbrella. She shoved books into her backpack and hurriedly made a couple of sandwiches. Rolling the sliding glass doors open, she trekked down her pathway to the beach, eager to beat Dean.

Dean hadn't even changed into board shorts and found his water socks yet when he heard a knock at his front door. He propped his board by the sliding doors. A few minutes ago, he'd heard Maribel's doors open, so it didn't make sense she was now knocking on his front door.

She must have forgotten something. Little miss perfect who wasn't so perfect in the end. But she was, as it turned out, his kind of perfection.

He swung the door open to find Amanda on the other side. *Amanda.* His vision grew hazy with confusion. Like being thrown from a horse, blinking, concussed and not certain what you were seeing was real. This shouldn't be happening now.

Wrong woman.

Amanda smiled and threw her arms around his neck. "It's true. You are here."

"Huh? But why are you here?" His arms automatically went around her elbows mostly to steady her and hold her a safe distance away.

"What do you mean?" She stepped back to give

him a long look, then smiled like she had a secret. "I heard you're making an offer. This was where you were going to go down on bended knee! That's what your real estate agent told me."

Damn. It was official. Today, he would fire his real estate agent.

"You have got to be kidding me. That was *before*. Way before."

She pushed past him, twirling in a circle, moving from room to room. "It's so lovely here, just like you said, and you were right. The perfect little vacation home for our future family. And we can turn the other units into places our rodeo friends can come and visit."

"Aren't you forgetting something, Amanda? We broke up. You didn't give me much choice when you cheated on me."

"I know how much I hurt you." She studied him from under hooded eyes. "But I thought I was forgiven."

"What in the world made you think that?" He crossed his arms.

"Because you're still going to buy these units. And if you hated me, if we were really *done*, you wouldn't even want to be here. Too many reminders."

As usual, Amanda saw no one but herself in any scenario.

"That's where you're wrong. You were never here with me, and I haven't thought about you once. You're not the be-all and end-all of everything. You never were," he stated for good measure, because it hadn't taken him long to realize this. "Don't forget, I grew up not far from here."

"I know. I know everything about you, Dean. We're perfect for each other, everybody says so."

"You mean *Rodeo Today* said so. And in case you've forgotten, I quit the rodeo." He hooked a thumb to his chest.

Interesting how the words no longer sent a jolt of anxiety through him. He had a lot more ready to take the place of rodeo, and he didn't mean his obsession with surfing.

"You quit after we broke up. I'll always feel that you lost your focus because of us. Because of me and what I'd done. I know I screwed up, but did it ever occur to you that I'd wanted you to quit the lifestyle a long time ago? I wanted to get married and have babies. But I supported you. I nursed you through injuries and took care of you."

But he hadn't lost his focus because of Amanda's screwup, as she had mentioned. The injuries had slowed him down, his stats weren't what they used to be. Amanda having turned to someone brighter, shinier and younger like Anton was just the finer point.

"You took care of me until you took care of Anton."

"He meant nothing to me! Did it ever occur to you I got tired of seeing you hurt? I wanted you to quit so we could live a normal life. We both wanted a family and kids. A ranch in Hill Country." She reached for his hands, took them in her own. "Honey, we were made for each other. You know we were."

Once, he'd actually believed that, too. It was amazing how much could change in a few months. He'd stepped back from the rodeo and found an entirely new world. It didn't include former rodeo queens, either. Not for him.

"Nope. We were *never* right for each other. It just worked out we had similar interests and lived in the same world. But if you take that world away, we have nothing at all."

Amanda chewed on her lower lip, the famous red puckered lip that made her as close to a cover model as anyone he'd ever met. She was beautiful, no doubt, and he'd been proud to be seen with her on his arm at one time. Back when all that mattered to him were appearances and position. Winning and achieving in his career. Doing whatever it took to get there. She'd never once asked him to quit the rodeo. Never once mentioned kids. He was the one who'd wanted kids but, holy rodeo, thank God he didn't have any with her.

Amanda brought on the tears, which in his opinion, she could manufacture as the need arose. She wasn't a bad person. Just a lost one. And definitely not the woman he loved.

Not even close.

"Please. I made a mistake, and I know you've always believed in second chances. You're the kind of person who forgives. The type of man who believes in love. I've seen it time and again."

True enough. He'd forgiven his mother when he shouldn't have, and maybe that had opened him up to the users of the world. Like Amanda. Anton, who he'd mentored at one time. But then again, as the old saying went, forgiveness was one thing. Forgetting was another.

"Look." He held up his palms to ward off the crying in any way he could. "I forgive you, Amanda. That *doesn't* mean I love you."

"And *I* don't believe you can turn it off so easily. You loved me once, I know it's true. Can't we at least talk?"

She sat on the couch, and in his experience, she wouldn't leave easily.

He thought of Maribel waiting for him on the beach. *Their* beach. She'd have the umbrella up by now and be sitting under it, reading a book. Possibly smiling. Waiting for him. He wanted to be there more than anywhere else in the world, and that included on a surfboard. But he didn't want Maribel meeting Amanda, and he didn't want Amanda and her wildly competitive nature to meet Maribel. There might be explosions. Maribel would slay Amanda with her superior intellect, which would be nice to see. But not terribly kind.

It was true Amanda had nursed him through many injuries, understood the circuit, was always his advocate.

"Not here," he said.

"Anywhere you'd like."

"Wait," he ordered. "I'll be back, and then we'll leave. Go to the bar or anywhere else. I'll listen, but don't expect me to change my mind."

"All I want is a chance to explain." She clasped her hands prayerfully.

Maybe he owed her *something* after all their time together. He could listen. They'd have closure, as Maribel called it.

But it wouldn't change a thing.

Maribel knew something was wrong the minute Dean stalked out to her without his trusty board under his arm. He hadn't changed into his board shorts, but still wore the jeans he had on this morning and had thrown on a tee.

She smiled and stood up from where she'd set up the umbrella again, all on her own, thank you very much.

"What's wrong?"

He surprised her by sitting under the umbrella. "Amanda showed up. My ex. She's not going to leave until I let her say her piece. So I'm going to let her talk. And then I'll get rid of her."

Fear gripped Maribel. Amanda. Amanda, the rodeo queen, the woman who'd been at Dean's side for years. The woman who had everything in common with him and also happened to be preternaturally beautiful.

"A-Amanda? Oh."

"I figure maybe I should listen to whatever she has to say."

No. She wholeheartedly disagreed. He shouldn't listen to anything a woman who cheated on him had to say.

But this was Dean, after all, who gave people chances even when they didn't necessarily deserve them. She loved this quality about him in about equal parts to her hatred of it. Maribel was right. Some people just didn't deserve a second chance.

"But…she cheated on you."

"It's true that I'd stopped paying her any real attention. Mostly I ignored her. All I cared about was the rodeo."

"That's not why you *cheat* on someone. You talk, you get counseling. You have a plan. You work things out because you care. Cheating is a red flag. It's a plan to blow up your life."

He almost smiled as his gaze drifted to the water and a sailboat drifting in the distance. "Listen to you, Dr. Del Toro."

She winced at the mention of her professional name as if he were *already* distancing himself. From her. Just like he'd done with Brianna.

"I won't be gone long." He stood and walked off without giving her a kiss.

Without a hug. Without a smile.

He was just…gone.

Everybody deserves a second chance.

Nothing can overcome love.

All things Dean had said to her that now resonated as loudly as the crashing waves. She'd wanted that kind of love and devotion, but someone else had been there first. He'd loved Amanda once, and even her cheating wouldn't overcome his love. It was wrong, but he wouldn't see it clearly through his fog. He'd forgive. A woman like Amanda would use every tool in her rodeo queen arsenal to get him back. And he'd give her a second chance because, c'mon, this was *Dean*, who believed in people the way Maribel did not.

She believed in books. Dean's retreating back got farther and farther away from her, and Maribel turned away. She settled under the umbrella and went back to her story.

Ignore. Ignore. Ignore the grumpy surfer who wound himself around your heart.

In her current read, a happily ever after was guaranteed. She saw it happening when she turned the pages and felt the pounding of the actor hero's heart as he ran down the streets of the city, chasing after the dog walker heroine, deeply regretting his stupid man-child actions. Maribel's heart swelled as she accepted his grand gesture of giving her not just any gift but *the* gift.

She closed the book, her finger slid down the spine, and she sighed.

Maybe not for her, but happily ever after happened in real life, too. Sometimes. Witness Jordan and Rafe, for instance. Max and Ava. All of *their* friends. But Maribel was too smart for all that. When she couldn't see what lay straight ahead of her, she wouldn't take that leap of faith.

Dean had walked away from her today and the message was clear. He likely wouldn't be back. She wasn't going to sit around and wait for him. She wasn't going to cry. She absolutely, 100 percent *refused*. Let that be some other heroine. In her book, Maribel Del Toro, PhD, was way too smart for that.

So she closed up her umbrella and grabbed her books, hiking back up to the cottage. Alone.

Hours later, Dean still hadn't returned, and yes, she was watching the clock. Hopelessly still filled with hope, but yeah. Not a big shock. *Wonder if he got them a hotel room in town.* He wouldn't want to shove their reunion right in Maribel's face. No matter what else she could say about Dean, he wasn't cruel. Not even a little bit. He'd spare her the view of Amanda as she got him back. As he gave her a second chance. She was fairly certain he'd come back at some point, probably before he left, to say goodbye and thank her for a good time.

To ask for her understanding as he tried to find his closure and find a way to make it work. She hated the fact it all made logical sense. After all, real love took time to grow and flourish, the kind of time he'd enjoyed with his ex. Even if she and Dean had experienced a sort of relationship trial by fire, what they had couldn't be replaced by years of building a relationship. Years of investing time and energy. It would be tough to throw it all away, and even she could see that.

Well, time to get the heck out of here. Her days on the beach were numbered. She'd go home earlier than planned, accept the offer and throw herself into her work. Tomorrow, she'd call about changing her ticket.

As for the rest of today, Valerie and Cole *had* said she was welcome anytime at the lighthouse, and this was as good a day as any other. She didn't want to be next door to notice that Dean never came home and had spent the night somewhere else. *With* someone else.

When she got to the lighthouse, she noticed an unusual number of cars parked around the driveway. She thought twice about knocking, worrying she was intruding on some type of celebration. Then she saw Patsy Villanueva walking back up the pathway from her vehicle with her cane.

She waved. "Hello, mija! Are you here for the poetry reading?"

Oh, Lord. Poetry reading? Valerie had said they still hosted the Almost Dead Poets Society on occasion, but she hadn't mentioned this particular night. Mostly they met at the bookstore where they were more than welcome. But now, Maribel was trapped. She could turn around and run out of here with some excuse about having left the stove on, but what if she ran into Dean and Amanda?

Patsy's expectant and glassy eyes reminded her of her grandmother's.

Hopeful. Believing.

And Maribel never liked to let her abuelita down.

"Sure." Maribel hiked the rest of the way up the path and met Patsy. "What are you sharing with everyone tonight?"

She held up a lined piece of paper. "Something new. So new I haven't even memorized it yet. But honestly, it's my best one. Sometimes it comes to me that way. This is something very special. Oh, you're going to love it."

"I'm sure I will."

Although, tonight, not so much. Patsy's poems verged on the erotic, and this wasn't a place Maribel wanted her mind wandering to at the moment. In fact, she was about ready to drop by Once Upon a Book and hand over all her money for all those ugly-cry books. She'd read one on the plane, cry her heart out, and when someone asked her what was wrong, she'd hold up the cover and blame the author.

Maribel opened the front door and waited for Patsy to walk inside. In no time at all, she was assaulted with greetings from the senior set.

"Is that Maribel Del Toro?" shouted Mr. Finch. "Come on in, child."

"Maribel, sweetheart." Lois greeted her and wrapped her in a hug.

Susannah and Ella Mae were right behind her, dispensing hugs and love. And damn if it wasn't just what she needed tonight. A little bit of home. She'd only met these people a few months ago at Max's wedding, and yet they treated her like another grand-daughter. Maribel had never lacked for family, but since coming to Charming, she'd come to understand the theory behind a found family.

The smells of cooked pork and chicken assaulted her senses. On top of everything else, she'd neglected to notice it was dinnertime. And here she'd shown up like a stray dog asking to be fed. Ugh.

"I'm sorry about tonight," Valerie whispered, little Wade hanging on her hip. "It was kind of last-minute."

"I'm the one who's sorry. You don't have to feed me. I didn't realize this was a dinner party."

"Oh, it's not. Honestly? Cooking gives me something to do and a way to ignore my grandma's poems without being rude. When it's her turn, I always have to get up and stir something."

Wade blew her a raspberry, saliva rolling down his chin, reminding Maribel so much of Brianna that her heart tugged.

"Oops. Sorry again, that's something new. He seems to have just discovered he can make these sounds on command. It's not a lot of fun, but he is kind of adorable." Valerie wiped at his chin and kissed his little cheek.

"He sure is." She was just about to stroke his sweet baby-soft skin with the back of her hand when Valerie unceremoniously handed him over.

Wade blinked in surprise, but like his father, he was a friendly sort. He gave her a smile, then lowered his head almost shyly.

"Aw, look at that. Like his father, he's a big flirt." She patted Wade's back. "Do you mind? Cole is busy with the grill, and I need to frost the cake."

"Cake? Hold on a second here. You have *cake*?" Maybe this night wouldn't be a complete heartache. She always had room for cake.

"I do. And it's chocolate." Valerie laughed and walked into the open kitchen to join Cole.

The lighthouse never failed to amaze Maribel with its winding staircase restored from an old ship. Windows were portholes, and the teak wood floors gleamed. Upstairs were two bedrooms and a deck that housed an old-fashioned telescope such as the type used in the old working lighthouses.

Maribel readjusted Wade in her arms, noting how much heavier he was than Brianna. She missed that little girl and her smiles, kicks of excitement and fist circles. Was she doing okay tonight with Tammy? Were her grandparents ecstatic to see her? Were any of them holding her the way Dean had, like a football, to help with the gas? Were they carrying her in the front pack the way Dean had, giving her a view of the world?

Were they singing to her the way Maribel had?

"Sit here by me, mija." Patsy patted the spot beside her on the couch.

Maribel settled down, shifting Wade to her knee,

bouncing him a little. He seemed to love it immediately.

"You're so good with children," Patsy said. "He likes you."

She listened to the poetry readings, one of the persistent themes being books, appropriate since they were all worried about the bookstore in town. Ella Mae went on and on about the importance of the written word, Mr. Finch discussed at length how e-books would never replace the printed word, so help him God, and Susannah had written another poem about her dog, Doodle.

Then Patsy stood and went to the center of the room.

Susannah clapped. "All right, let's hear it, Patsy. I'm in the mood for love."

"Yes, it's about love. But not how you might think." She pointed with authority.

She then launched into a lyrical poem about the love between a parent and a child. The only love that existed before two people ever met. The only circle of love that could never be broken. Unconditional and unwavering. She smiled at Wade as she recited it, also meeting Valerie's and Cole's eyes.

Everyone clapped, but no one louder than Valerie, who hugged her grandmother. "Thank you."

"This one just came to me. Next week I'll go back to my regular steamy reads." Patsy waved her hand dismissively. "Don't worry. I know that's my thing."

The tears rolled down Maribel's face before she

realized her eyes were watery. If she'd only realized they were imminent, she would have held them back. But they'd just slid out of her eyes like they suddenly ran the show.

Wade turned to give her a look that said, *Who are you again?* He fussed and Cole swiftly took him out of Maribel's arms.

"Oh, no. Honey, are you okay?" Patsy said, rubbing Maribel's back.

"It's your poem, Patsy." Lois sniffed. "So touching and heartfelt."

"I know, but even I'm not *that* talented."

Suddenly Maribel was surrounded by senior citizens who were ready to dispense hugs and tissues.

"I just miss my family, I think."

And by family, she had a sudden and unbidden picture in her mind of Dean and Brianna. The three of them sleeping together during a storm. But that family was temporary and gone. Brianna was back where she belonged and so was Dean.

"Oh, mija. Think of me as your family," Patsy said, wrapping her arms around Maribel.

And Maribel cried a little harder then.

Somehow, she got through dinner with the gang, shockingly only taking two bites of cake. She slowly drove back to the cottages, taking her time, because it was now dark outside with only the stars and full moon to guide her way. As she pulled up, the sight in front of her made her heart sink.

This couldn't be happening. Not again.

There was a *basket* at her doorstep. A basket, like the one Brianna had been abandoned in. She couldn't get out of the car fast enough, but when she reached the basket, it was empty. Empty, that is, save for red grapes, chocolate, crackers, cheese and a bottle of wine.

What in the world?

Then Dean emerged from next door, looking the grumpiest she'd seen him since the day he carried her bag inside.

"What *this*?" She picked up the basket.

"Where were you?" he demanded.

"Where was I? *Where was I?* Where were *you*?"

"You know where. I told you. But when I got here, you were gone with no note. Nothing."

"Dean, you were gone for hours. I'm supposed to think you weren't going to reconcile with Amanda? It seemed clear to me that was your plan!"

He lowered his head, shook it and studied her from under hooded eyes. "Wow. No, that was never part of the plan. Never."

"But you said—"

"Weren't you the one who mentioned 'closure'? I was going to hear her out."

"I know what that means. She was going to ask for forgiveness, for a second chance. And you were going to give it to her because that's who you are."

He took a step toward her, then another.

"Wrong. But actually, it isn't always the offense itself that is or isn't forgivable so much as the person. She asked me whether I could ever forgive her and start over from the beginning. And, actually, a part of me thought maybe I could."

Maribel shook her head as her heart split. "I don't need to hear this."

"I still believe people deserve second chances. And I will always believe that."

"Noted."

"But love always has to be a part of it. Forgiveness doesn't just happen in a vacuum. You need to start with love. And… I don't love her anymore. You were right. She blew it up, and there must have been a reason. We were never right for each other. Just in the same world at the same time."

Maribel wasn't sure she heard right, but nevertheless her stupid heart slammed into her rib cage. Amanda was gorgeous and penitent, and maybe she'd never cheat again. She also had a lot in common with Dean. More than Maribel would ever have.

"But you two have so much history together. I know how much family means to you, and maybe on some level, she was your family for a while."

He shook his head. "None of that matters when our hearts just don't align together."

Maribel had nothing to say to that. He didn't love Amanda. Okay. He'd sent the rodeo queen away. This did not compute. It was completely illogical.

Quite possibly a little bit like love. The fireworks. Kablammy. The almost nonsensical call of two hearts who were drawn to each other like magnets.

"We… You and I don't have much in common."

He took the last step to bridge the distance between them. "We have the three Bs, and we will always have that."

"We're already missing one of them." She shook her head, thinking of the sweet little baby that owned her heart. "And when we leave here, we won't have the beach, either."

"Maribel, I'm going to tell you something right now, and I don't want you to get upset."

"Oh boy, that's not a good way to begin a sentence."

But he reached for her hand and took it in his own. "I haven't told you something about me because it never came up and didn't seem important at the time. Still isn't, but I'm only telling you now because it has to do with what we're talking about."

"Uh-huh," she stuttered, wondering where this could be leading.

He swallowed noticeably, lowered his gaze then met her eyes.

"I have quite a bit of money I've socked away over the years. When you're poor, you worry you'll never see money again. So I saved, invested and bought land, champion horses for breeding. Stock and bonds. I'm smarter than I look. I came here to check out these cottages as an investment. That's why they were mostly empty. Except for yours."

"Okay," she said slowly, still not knowing why he was telling her this right here and now.

"What I'm telling you is that I'm buying this beach house."

"This one?" She threw a glance at her door.

"No, I mean *all* of them."

"All of them."

The place where they'd first met, argued, joined together to care for a baby and, at least on her part, fallen in love.

"You bought our beach?" She felt her lips quiver and pulled them into a smile.

"It's our thing, and I don't want anyone else to have it." He grinned. "And we can come back here this summer, next year, anytime you want. I fell in love with you here, and I'll always want to come back here. Just you and me."

She'd still been reeling from the "we" in his sentence when he said he loved her. He'd chosen her, and she'd done nothing but simply open up her heart. Nothing would ever compare to this feeling of utter euphoria. It was a little like flying.

"I love you, too." She fisted his shirt, pulling him closer.

"That's good, because it turns out I kind of have a thing for smart girls." He glanced at the basket on the step she'd almost forgotten. "I got the basket to make a point. This time there isn't a baby we need to rescue. There isn't arguing and figuring out what to do with a baby while terrified we're going to screw it all up. We did this whole relationship thing backwards. Started with the baby and all the tough stuff.

If we handled that, we could do anything together. And I think it's time we get to the good part. To be in love, act goofy, piss each other off and kiss and make up."

"I love the sound of that. Especially the making up part."

"Don't worry, we'll still fight. And I'm really good at makeup sex. Even better than the shower." He winked.

"And that's saying something."

She kissed him, then swung the door wide-open and invited him inside.

Epilogue

Eighteen months later

Maribel smiled and stepped out of the Land Rover, memories flooding her.

"Sweetheart, six suitcases? *Seriously?*" Dean complained, hauling each one to the front door of the beach rental. "We're only here a week."

He'd been a little grumpy today because after hurting his shoulder at the ranch a few months ago, he'd been instructed to lay off surfing, too. And being here in Charming and *not* surfing was going to be hell on her cowboy.

"One suitcase is filled with our books, and another one has all those clothes we bought for Brianna."

They planned to visit Brianna and Tammy in

Houston, because other than frequent photos, neither one of them had seen the baby since they'd both left Charming over a year ago. But Dean kept in touch with both Tammy and her parents, receiving frequent updates on Brianna, who had started to crawl. *Crawl!* Maribel could hardly wait to see her again. Photos showed she grew prettier every day. Tammy had enrolled in cosmetology and hairstyling classes, planning to move into her own place early next year. Using some of his former contacts, Dean had arranged for her to do hair and makeup for some of those rodeo queens.

They'd planned to visit them earlier, but these rental units were in high demand and were solidly booked all summer long. They'd been busy anyway since Maribel decided to start over. After several trips to Hill Country to see Dean, she'd fallen in love with the area as quickly as she'd fallen in love with the man himself. So, three months into her new position as a psychologist for the medical clinic in Watsonville, she'd given notice. Maribel then moved to the tiny town of Lovelock, Texas, to be with Dean and, a few months ago, hung out her shingle: *Maribel Del Toro-Hunter, PhD*.

She had a tiny office in the middle of town and was the only counselor for miles, which meant she handled it all. She mostly worked as a liaison for their tiny two-man police department. Troubled teens were her specialty.

Yes, her family *had* been a little shell-shocked

by all the sweeping changes, but once they'd met Dean, they understood. Mami, in particular, was convinced at least maybe there was one more vaquero that proved to be the exception to the rule. And when he went down on bended knee and proposed in front of her entire family, they officially declared him a son forever. Her family adored him, and he called them Mami and Papi like they were his own. If Dean had ever lacked family, he had his own now in spades.

He'd told her that having a family he now considered his own had made his acceptance of the end of his rodeo career easier to handle. Now, he had fully thrown himself into his cattle ranch and was at the forefront of using environmentally friendly methods.

Their marriage happened rather quickly, like the way they fell in love. Even now, changes were afoot, and Maribel sometimes worried she'd taken on too much too soon. But then she'd look at Dean, and all her doubts would fade. He made her laugh every day and constantly surprised her. She had no doubt she'd love him forever.

Once inside the cottage, Maribel drew back the curtains, slid open the glass doors and took in a deep breath of the salty fresh air. The sandy well-worn path to their beach was the same beautiful view that had changed her life.

"Are you feeling okay?" Dean came up behind her, wrapping his arms around her swollen belly.

She was four months along now and had begun

to show. Leaning back into his embrace, she assured him she was fine. The first trimester had been a mini disaster, with Maribel sick every morning and unable to hold much food down. Dean was so worried he called the doctor twice a day and made an absolute nuisance of himself. But this wasn't the first challenge they'd weathered, and it wouldn't be the last. They were still a good team in every sense of the word.

As for Amanda, Maribel had later learned that she'd preyed on Dean's kindness all those months ago. She'd kept him away for hours, and when nothing worked, she talked him into buying her a ticket to fly home. In tears, she'd then begged him to drive her to the airport, which he did and waited until her flight boarded. Because…he was Dean, after all. Good and kind, giver of second chances.

He believed nothing could conquer love and in no time at all, he'd convinced her it was true.

"I'm looking forward to a lot of reading under my umbrella this week."

"Ditto."

Dean was currently reading a sci-fi book, because her adrenaline junkie of a husband preferred more action. And he'd found that the quiet and the calm and peace of her light romance novels were no longer needed. He usually slept like a log right next to her, sleepless nights apparently gone forever. Or at least until their own baby arrived.

Romance books still worked for her and always

would. Even if she was no longer looking to escape from her own reality, taking a trip into someone else's imaginary world was peaceful and calming.

As long as you had the right book.

Much the same as life, and love, when you chose the right man.

* * * * *

You'll love these other uplifting titles from Heatherly Bell:

A Charming Christmas Arrangement
The Charming Checklist
Winning Mr. Charming
Grand Prize Cowboy
More than One Night
Reluctant Hometown Hero
The Right Moment

Available from Harlequin Special Edition!

#3007 FALLING FOR DR. MAVERICK

Montana Mavericks: Lassoing Love • by Kathy Douglass

Mike Burris and Corinne Hawkins's rodeo romance hit the skids when Mike pursued his PhD. But when the sexy doctor-in-training gets word of Corrine's plan to move on without him, he'll pull out all the stops to kick-start their flatlined romance.

#3008 THE RANCHER'S CHRISTMAS REUNION

Match Made in Haven • by Brenda Harlen

Celebrity Hope Bradford broke Michael Gilmore's heart years ago when she left to pursue her Hollywood dreams. The stubborn rancher won't forgive and forget. But when Hope is forced to move in with him on his ranch—and proximity gives in to lingering attraction—her kisses thaw even the grinchiest heart!

#3009 SNOWBOUND WITH A BABY

Dawson Family Ranch • by Melissa Senate

When a newborn baby is left on Detective Reed Dawson's desk with a mysterious note, he takes in the infant. But social worker Aimee Gallagher has her own plans for the baby...until a snowbound weekend at Reed's ranch challenges all of Aimee's preconceived notions about family and love.

#3010 LOVE AT FIRST BARK

Crimson, Colorado • by Michelle Major

Cassie Raebourn never forgot Aiden Riley—or the way his loss inspired her to become a veterinarian. Now the shy boy is a handsome, smoldering cowboy, complete with bitterness and bluster. It's Cassie's turn to inspire Aiden...with adorable K-9 help!

#3011 A HIDEAWAY WHARF HOLIDAY

Love at Hideaway Wharf • by Laurel Greer

Archer Frost was supposed to help decorate a nursery—not deliver Franci Walker's baby! She's smitten with the retired coast guard diver, despite his gruff exterior. He's her baby's hero...and hers. Will Franci's determined, sunny demeanor be enough for Archer to realize *he's* their Christmas miracle?

#3012 THEIR CHRISTMAS RESOLUTION

Sisters of Christmas Bay • by Kaylie Newell

Stella Clarke will stop at nothing to protect her aging foster mother. But when sexy real estate developer Ian Steele comes to town with his sights set on her Victorian house, Stella will have to keep mistletoe and romance from softening her hardened holiday reserve!

HARLEQUIN
PLUS

Try the best multimedia subscription service for romance readers like you!

Read, Watch and Play.

Experience the easiest way to get the romance content you crave.

Start your **FREE TRIAL** at
<u>www.harlequinplus.com/freetrial</u>.